Also by Elizabeth Berg
Available from Random House Large Print

**The Story of Arthur Truluv**
**Once Upon a Time, There Was You**

# Night of Miracles

# Night of Miracles

A NOVEL

## Elizabeth Berg

RANDOM HOUSE
LARGE PRINT

Published in the United States of America by Random House Large Print in association with Random House, a division of Penguin Random House LLC, New York.

Grateful acknowledgment is made to The Permissions Company, Inc., on behalf of Copper Canyon Press for permission to reprint "Painting the Barn" from **Splitting an Order** by Ted Kooser, copyright © 2014 by Ted Kooser. Reprinted with the permission of The Permissions Company, Inc., on behalf of Copper Canyon Press, www.coppercanyonpress.org.

Cover illustration: Ben Perini

The Library of Congress has established a Cataloging-in-Publication record for this title.

ISBN: 978-0-525-63178-1

www.penguinrandomhouse.com/large-print-format-books

FIRST LARGE PRINT EDITION

Printed in the United States of America

10  9  8  7  6  5  4  3  2  1

This Large Print edition published in accord with the standards of the N.A.V.H.

In memory of Homer, still here

The ghost of my good dog, Alice,
sits at the foot of my ladder,
looking up, now and then touching
the bottom rung with her paw.
Even a spirit dog can't climb
an extension ladder, and so,
with my scraper, bucket, and brush,
I am up here alone, hanging on
with one hand in the autumn wind,
high over the earth that Alice
knew so well, every last inch,
and there she sits, whimpering
in just the way the chilly wind
whines under the tin of the roof—
sweet Alice, dear Alice, good Alice,
waiting for me to come down.

—"Painting the Barn," from
   **Splitting an Order** by Ted Kooser

Night of Miracles

Surely you've had this happen. You are seated by choice or misfortune in a window seat on an airplane. You look out as the plane takes off, rises up higher and higher, levels off. If you chance to glance down, you see a particular kind of order not realized on earth. You might feel a kind of hopefulness at the sight of houses clustered together in their various neighborhoods, at roads running straight or artfully curved, at what look like toy cars. You see the lakes and rivers, occasionally the wide stretch of ocean meeting horizon. You see natural quilts formed by the lay of fields and farmlands, you see the grouping of trees into parks and forests. Sometimes you see the splendor of autumn leaves or Fourth of July fireworks. Or sunsets. Or sunrises.

All of this can inspire something unnameable but nearly graspable, a kind of yearning toward a grand possibility.

And then you land.

But what if you landed differently?

# Diamonds in a Box

―

AFTER SHE HAS DRIED AND PUT AWAY HER SUP-per dishes, Lucille Howard sits at her kitchen table and contemplates what to do with another empty evening. A few years back, she might have sat out on the front porch with her former neighbor and then roommate, Arthur Moses, a man too good of heart for this world, in Lucille's opinion, though she and many others profited plenty from his continual kindness.

She pushes herself up from the table and goes out onto her front porch to stand with her hands on her hips, taking in a better view of the night sky. From the kitchen window the stars are so clear they look like diamonds; out here, it's even more glorious.

As a child, Lucille thought stars **were** diamonds, and that if only she prayed in the right way, the cigar box she kept under her bed would be filled with them some morning, and she could make a necklace out of them. Never happened. Well, of course it never happened, stars are not diamonds. They're suns, really, just balls of gas. If there's one thing Lucille hates, it's how science has to rain on whimsy's parade: Rainbows not a gift from leprechauns offering pots of gold, but only a trick of refraction. A blue sky not a miles-wide painting done by a heavenly hand, but molecules scattering light. Still, when Lucille sees the stars strewn across the sky on a night like tonight, they're diamonds, and she thinks they might end up under her bed yet. Maybe she'll put a box back under there. Tradition. Whimsy. Hope. Magical thinking, oh, she knows it's magical thinking; and she knows, too, that she's more prone to it now than she ever was. But what fun to imagine kneeling down to lift the dust ruffle and just check. And there they are at last, diamonds in a box, shining so hard they light up the surprised oval of her face.

It's cold enough for a jacket, this being the first of October, but Lucille is still in the habit of summer (the roses still blooming!) and so has neglected to put one on. It feels like too much work to go back in and get one, so she settles into a rocking chair, wraps her arms around herself, and moves vigorously back and forth. There. That's fine. It's good for you to be a bit uncomfortable from time to time, especially if you're only a few steps away from relief. People forget about the value of adversity. It was something she always tried to teach her fourth-grade students, how adversity can strengthen character. She also tried to teach them the value of having to work for something instead of it being handed to you the instant you said you wanted it. That's what happens these days, no one waits for anything. But Lucille used to give her class construction-paper coupons with points for good behavior or for scholastic merit; and when they had enough points, she'd bake them a little baby pie in a five-inch tin, whatever kind they wanted, and they got to keep the tin. They'd loved that. Once, a boy named Danny Matthews had wanted to cut his pie up so that everyone in the twenty-three-pupil class could have some. That had been a good lesson in mathematics. Danny was one of those kids who was never much liked, no matter how hard he tried. He was a very clumsy boy (the kids called him Mr. Magoo for the way he tripped over and bumped into things), and perpetually disheveled. Well, Lucille liked him and his crooked grin, and he **loved** her—he might act up with others, but he always listened to her. She heard he'd enlisted and gotten killed in Afghanistan.

It was true what they told her on the first day of teachers' college: you never forget some of your students. For Lucille, it was the cut-ups she could never keep from laughing at, the dreamers she had to keep reeling back into the classroom, and little Danny Matthews, with his ragged heart of gold.

Lucille gives herself a challenge: she'll stay out here until it feels like her teeth might chatter. Then she'll go inside, draw a bath, and have a soak in Epsom salts. One thing she's grateful for are the grab bars she's had installed, though even with them, getting herself down into the tub is a herculean task that reminds her a bit of elephants lowering themselves onto tiny stools, the way they used to have to do in the circus. She's glad no one can see her, the way she grunts and huffs and puffs. **Lord!** they would say. **Why don't you switch to showers? You're eighty-eight!** True, but mostly she feels like she's sixty-eight. When she was sixty-eight, she felt like she was forty-eight. And so, although she knows the logic is off, she tells everyone that she feels forty-eight.

Lucille will not give up her baths. No. In the tub, she is what she thinks being stoned must be like: she enjoys a feeling of timelessness and wide content. A float-y, perfumed detachment. After her bath, she'll read her Maeve Binchy book, and then she'll go to sleep.

Maeve Binchy died young. Seventy-two. Lucille bets there are seventy-two-year-olds who can still do the splits. If she could have given Maeve Binchy a year from her own life, you can bet she'd have done it. She actually cried when Maeve Binchy died; she sat in a kitchen chair and twisted a Kleenex in her hands and cried, and she felt a little tornado of frustration in her midsection because there was **another** good one, gone too soon.

Well, bath and bed and then another day will be done, and she'll be another step closer to the **exit grande.** She's not morbid, she's not sad, she's just a realist. She **is** closer to death. Everyone is, from the moment they slide out of the womb. From time to time, Lucille even feels a jazzy jump of joy, thinking about the journey to the place no one knows about, really, never mind the stories of the bright light and the tunnel and whatnot. No one really knows.

Just as she's ready to get up and go inside, she sees the neighbor who bought her old house, right next door to the smaller house she lives in now, which was Arthur's house. He willed it to Maddy Harris, the girl who used to live here with them, and Lucille now rents it from Maddy, if you call "rent" simply taking care of the place. The neighbor is coming out to walk his dog. Lucille has nothing against dogs, but that one is the ugliest thing she's ever seen. An ancient, mid-size gray mutt who looks like he needs a shave. Bugged-out eyes like a pug. A bit bowlegged. A tail that looks more like Eeyore's than a dog's. And his name: Henry. Now, why in the world would you give a dog that looks like that a name befitting a king?

"Hello, Lucille," the man calls over.

"Hello, Jason," Lucille answers, though she muffles the name a bit. **Is** it Jason? Or is it Jeremy? Or Jeffrey? It's a little past the point where she can ask; the neighbors have been there for almost a year. The **J.** person, his wife, Abby, and their ten-year-old son, whose name is . . . well, for heaven's sake. Starts with an **L.** Liam? Leroy? Lester?

She closes her eyes to concentrate. Lincoln! That's it. Another strange name, if you ask her. What's become of Spot and Rex and Champ for dogs?

What's become of Mary and Sally and Billy for children?

This is what happens. You live past your time of importance and relevance and the world must be given over to the younger ones. Lucille is all right with that notion. As the old folks yielded to her as a young woman, she will yield to the young folks coming up after her. But there is one thing she's going to get before she is here no more. And that is a very specific miracle, which she feels is owed her. In spades.

Lucille has kept her eyes closed and is startled now by the sound of footsteps: J. and his dog, coming up onto her porch. She cries out and leaps to her feet.

"Sorry," the man says. "Did I scare you?"

"Yes!"

"I'm sorry."

"It's all right." She pulls her hand down from where it had flown up onto her chest.

"I just wanted to ask you if you'd be free to come to our house for dinner tomorrow night. Abby's been meaning to ask you forever, but we—"

"Tomorrow night? What time?"

"Seven?"

"Seven! How can your son wait that long to eat?"

"Six?" the man asks, smiling.

"That's better."

"Okay, good, we'll see you then." J. pulls at the leash, but Henry apparently has no interest in going anywhere. He stares up at Lucille as though he's forgotten something in her house and won't leave without retrieving it.

"Run along now, Henry," Lucille says. "Obey your master."

The dog moves closer to her, sniffs at her toes, then at the hem of her pants. "I was just going in . . ." she says, and Henry barks: once, twice, excitedly.

Lucille puts her hands on her knees and bends toward the dog. "What is it, girl?" she asks. "Is Gramps in trouble?" She looks up at J., grinning.

The man stares at her blankly.

"**Lassie**?" Lucille says.

"Who's that?"

"A show that used to be on TV? About a collie dog? And his boy, Timmy?"

"Ah," J. says. "Right." He pulls harder at the leash and the dog finally comes to him. "See you tomorrow."

"I'll bring dessert," Lucille says. She has some cake left over from the last class she taught. Her baking classes have been getting so popular that she recently put an ad in the local paper to hire some help.

The man turns around. "Uh, we don't . . . I hope this doesn't offend you, but we don't eat dessert."

Lucille cannot think of one thing to say, but finally manages a stiff "I see." And here is a bit of a miracle right now, because what she really, really thought she'd say is, "Never mind, then. I don't want to come."

They're probably vegans. They'll probably have a

square loaf of some brownish mass on an ugly pot-
tery platter and a bunch of vegetables so barely
cooked they're next to raw. Lucille will put a potpie
in her oven before she goes over, so she can eat when
she gets home.

She goes inside, and the warmth of her house
settles around her. **Come here, dearie,** says the
kitchen. **Come and have a nice slice of cake.**

She does exactly that. Yellow cake with milk-
chocolate frosting, a classic, but if you use Lucille's
recipe for yellow cake and buttercream (Southern, of
course) it's a bit more than a classic. It's a table-
pounder. It's a groaner. "Oh, my goodness, this is
**five stars!**" said a woman who took the class, after
she tasted the cake. "Six!" said another, her mouth
full, and Lucille has to agree. She never expected that
the adult response to her desserts would be more
enthusiastic than the kids'. But then for the young
children she teaches (ages five to seven, no older, no
younger, no exception), everything is still a wonder.
One day, teaching a fancied-up version of Rice
Krispies Treats, she had to compete for their attention with a squirrel that came to the kitchen window
to look in. The weather's another distraction. Let big
fat snowflakes fall, or thunder boom, or a sudden
wind whoosh through the trees, and she's lost the
entire class.

After Lucille eats the cake, she weighs herself in an
effort not to have a second slice. It does not work,
which she might have predicted, and so she does

have a second slice. Well, she finishes the cake. Maybe it's two and half slices. Maybe it's three.

She bathes, and she supposes it's having eaten all that cake that makes it even more difficult than usual to get out of the tub. Worth it.

She climbs into bed, reads for a while, then turns out the light. She lies flat on her back and stares at the ceiling, aware of a throbbing loneliness that comes over her from time to time. "Lucille Pearson," she says into the darkness. And then she says it again, more slowly, "Luciiiiillllle Peeeearson." Still not right. "Mrs. Frank Pearson," she says, quite briskly, even authoritatively. That's the one. That's how she would have said her name, if she'd had the opportunity.

This is the first time she's ever said out loud what she would have been saying for five years now, had she married him. The words make for a quick mix of emotions: First a zippy thrill, then a big ploppy sense of contentment, and it's like butter in a pan, that feeling of contentment, melting and spreading out inside her. Then a terrible bitterness, because she is not Mrs. Frank Pearson, nor will she ever be.

She sighs and turns onto her side. Tears slide down her cheeks and she wipes them away. She supposes she'll always cry over Frank: finding the first and only love of her life in high school and losing him, then finding him again—at eighty-three!—only to lose him again, to a heart attack, just like that. Here, then gone again. So very much here, then so very much gone.

She closes her eyes and tells herself to dream of him. Oftentimes, it works, telling herself to dream of someone, and her dreams are increasingly very real-seeming. After the death of her friend Arthur, she could summon him up on a regular basis. She dreamed of Arthur sitting on the porch with her, as he so often used to do, eating cookies, taking his tiny bites and brushing crumbs carefully into his hand. She dreamed he was out in the garden with his battered old straw hat on, pruning roses, the sun shining right through his stick-out ears when he turned to offer her an impromptu bouquet. Sometimes she dreamed he was laughing with Maddy.

Maddy had been eighteen and pregnant by her lousy ex-boyfriend when she moved in with Arthur to be his housekeeper. She and Arthur had met in the cemetery, where Arthur used to go every day to visit his wife, Nola, and where Maddy went to escape lunch hour—if not whole days—at her high school. What a fragile and sorrowful little being Maddy had been, a motherless child, estranged from her father, bullied in school, with absolutely no friends. But Arthur ("Truluv," Maddy had nicknamed him) took her into his home, and after a little while Lucille moved into Arthur's house, too. The girl needed proper nourishment, and a woman's touch, Lucille thought. And Lucille needed company. Now Maddy has just about finished college—she goes to a wonderful place very close by where she can keep her child with her in the dorm. She studies photography and she has started to become quite successful. More important, at least in Lucille's opinion, she's doing a great job raising her daughter, named Nola, after Arthur's wife. Lucille misses both Maddy and little Nola, but they keep in touch with cards and phone calls and the occasional visit. Nola's drawings wallpaper Lucille's kitchen: big-headed figures with crossed eyes and stick fingers, lines of sparse grass with perky flowers poking up, tilted houses with smoke coming out of chimneys, figure-eight cats.

Lucille's dreams of Arthur are always pleasant. Sometimes she asks to dream of him because she misses him. More often, it's for a particular kind of comfort. When her GERD is acting up, say, or if a news story has scared the bejesus out of her.

When she asks to dream of Frank, it's different. Her dreams of him are particularly intense. She can smell him; he always smelled of Old Spice and soap and leather, and if that isn't the best scent on earth, she doesn't know what is; it's even better than baking bread. She and Frank have conversations, too, and she hears his voice plain as day.

Well, she may have had Frank for just short of a month, but to Lucille it seemed like a little lifetime. In her dreams, she and Frank are together always, and even if they're not looking at each other, they're seeing each other. It would have been wonderful to spend the rest of their lives together, it would. Not just for the immense pleasure of being with each other but for the services they would have provided each other. Reminding each other to take their pills. Accompanying each other to doctors' appointments.

Helping each other decide whether to be buried or cremated—a lot of people think that's just an awful thing to talk about, but when you're old, you've got to. She thinks Frank would have made a joke.

Oh, he was wonderful, Frank, and the best thing was that he made her kind of wonderful, too. That is the gift of love, not only that you have somebody but that you are changed by somebody.

She will dream of Frank tonight, she can tell. She will feel she caught him by the tail of his spirit and he really is here, a see-through Frank come back to her. She will believe she is holding him tightly, running her hands up and down the personal mountain range of his spine, which she remembers perfectly, as she remembers everything about them being together, truly she does.

A letter on a random day from a man who last knew her when she was eighteen years old. Think of it. You're eighty-three, and your life has been stretched out like a rubber band. And then you open an envelope and **Snap!** there you are, back at eighteen. Eighteen inside of eighty-three. And you're ready for love just like you were all those years ago. Readier.

Lucille thinks she knows how most people would regard what happened between her and Frank. There was a time when she was in her late fifties and a woman from church, who was approaching ninety, told Lucille in a tremulous voice, "I still need love, too, you know." And Lucille felt a kind of embarrassment mixed with disdain, she must admit she felt some disdain. Because she believed the woman should be through with all that. What she knows now is that no one is ever through with love. No one ever should be.

These are the things Lucille thinks about before she falls asleep tonight. She is in her blue nightie and her hands are clasped between her knees and she is ready for Frank to come. When a deep pain snakes into her midsection, she ignores it. It will go away. It always does.

# Iris

I F YOU COULD LIVE ONE DAY IN YOUR LIFE over again and change the outcome of something that happened that day, what day would it be? This is a question many people have difficulty answering. Not Iris Winters. She knows the day, and she knows exactly how she'd change what happened.

Ten years ago, early morning. She was in bed, lying on her side, her eyes open. The drapes were cracked so that there was a thin band of sunlight running across her bent knees. She was staring dully ahead, breathing in, breathing out. The night before, she had told her husband, "I need to say something to you. And this is not a mood. I have thought carefully about this, and I am sure. I want a divorce, Ed. I don't want to have to say it again. Please don't make me say it again." She blinked back tears, lifted her chin. "I'm sorry."

Before he left for work, her husband came to sit on her side of the bed. He lowered himself onto the mattress very slowly, as if he were sore, or as if she were, or as if they both were. She moved only her eyes to look at him. He was wearing one of his good suits and the tie she liked best, a pale-blue silk with a paisley pattern. He took her hand in his, and his hand was sweaty: he was nervous. "Can we try again," he said. He didn't say it like a question, he said it like a statement. She took a while to answer. It was probably only a second or two, but it felt longer. And then she said, "No," in a morning voice that cracked. She cleared her throat and said it again: "No." No more anguished talks at the kitchen table, no more talks in front of television shows neither of them was really watching, no talks in the car, at restaurants, in bed at night. She was exhausted, and she was finished. She could not stop what she had started; it had its own momentum now, and all she wanted was for it to be over.

Her husband sat there for a minute, nodding. Then he said, "Would you be honest with me if I asked you just one thing?"

"What."

His voice was gentle, but firm. "Do you think that your pushing me so hard for something you wanted made me kind of necessarily resist it? Would you admit that, would you say that you pushed way too hard?"

She spoke with a cold remove. "No. I would not say that. I would say that I didn't push hard enough."

He nodded. "Okay. Well, I've been thinking. What if we—"

"No."

They didn't even eat together anymore, not breakfast, not lunch, not dinner. Oftentimes, they ate separate things, and Iris thought this was worse than separate beds. They were more than over. They were rotted.

Her husband stood and went out of the room, downstairs, and into the garage. He started his car, backed out, and drove off. Sounds she had heard thousands of times, but that day they were different.

If she could have the day back, it would go like this: She lets him finish asking the question. She sits up and puts the pillows behind her. Takes in a breath. She says, "Well, how would we do that?" And he tells her. And they do it. And it works. She stays. And she does not live every day for the next ten years with a small sword stuck into the back side of her heart.


AFTER SHE AND ED had been married for three years, Iris decided she was ready for a baby. She purchased a kit to check for pregnancy, she circled the days that month when they should be sure to have sex, she bought a hot-pink negligee that sat squarely between whimsical and sexy. That night, she said, "Guess what?"

After she'd told him, he said, "Wow. Well, let's see. Let's wait a bit."

"For what?" Iris asked.

"For . . . well, for one thing, let me have a little time to adjust to the idea."

"To the idea of . . . ?"

"Having kids!"

Iris stared at him. They were in the kitchen, he was sitting at the table chopping the ends off the green beans, she was turning the salmon in the marinade sauce. She resealed the ziplock bag, then came to sit at the table with him. She sat with her hands folded in her lap, a tight smile on her face.

"Did I forget to ask you something?"

He said nothing.

"Ed?"

"What."

"Did I make a wrong assumption?" The very thought made her feet feel cold.

"I don't know."

"I just . . . I mean, when we got married, I did assume you'd want children."

"But you never asked."

"And you never told, Ed! You never told me you didn't want children."

"I don't know if I don't want them **ever.** I just don't want them now."

"But . . . when, then?"

He pushed the cutting board away. "Jesus Christ, Iris. I don't **know**! I don't have an exact date for you!"

She swallowed, spoke quietly over a sudden dryness in her throat. "You like children. You seem to like children a lot."

"I do. But it doesn't mean I want any of my own."
He sighed and looked over at her. "My God, Iris,
look at the world."

She tilted her head and squinted at him. Her
mouth opened, but she said nothing.

"You know?" he said, getting up to wash his hands.
"Look at the environment. Look at the population
crisis."

"This . . . I have to tell you, this comes as a total
**shock** to me." She laughed. "I feel like I was putting
your underwear away and found a lethal weapon
in your drawer. I feel like . . . My God, Ed! I just had
no **idea** that we wouldn't have children. At least one.
Can't we have just one?"

"You sound like you're begging for a puppy."

"And you sound like a jerk."

Silence.

Then, "Ed. I was the girl who always minded her
egg. Remember in college when my psychology class
was doing that experiment with the eggs, you had to
care for your egg like it was your child? I took care of
the egg. Only one other girl and I, we didn't break
our eggs, we didn't lose them, we kept them with us
all the time."

"You didn't have your egg with you all the time."

"I did!"

"Not when we went out. I never saw it."

"It was in my purse. In a nest padded with flannel
that I made for it. I always had that egg."

"All right, so you were inordinately responsible for
an egg."

"And when I was a little girl, I played dolls incessantly. I asked for a rocker so I could rock them to sleep. I gave them illnesses so I could cure them. I cut out food from magazines to feed them. I checked on them in the night. I washed their clothes and laid them out on the lawn to dry. Ed! I **love** children! I want one of my own!"

Ed looked down. "I don't know, I guess we both made false assumptions. But just give me some time. Don't keep at this, okay? Let's think what this would mean, having children. Children aren't dolls, or eggs. Think about how they would impact our lives. How we could no longer do a lot of things we do now."

**I'm done doing those things**, she thought.

"Let's keep using birth control for another year, okay? And then we'll see."

"I don't want to take birth control pills anymore."

"Why not?"

"I've had some weird circulation things happening."

"Really? This isn't just an excuse?"

"Really, Ed. I'll get an IUD."

They ate dinner with an odd formality, as though they were on a first date.

That night, in bed, he pulled her to him, wrapped his arms around her, rested his chin on the top of her head, and told her he was sorry, but he thought they should both be sure. They'd talk about it again in a year.

She said one more thing. She said, "So, would you feel any differently about adoption?"

He said this: "Iris."

Finally, she let it go. They did have time. She was only in her late thirties. But then she got a terrible infection from the IUD, a life-threatening infection, one that necessitated a hysterectomy. After the surgery, when she woke up, Ed was by her bedside and he took her hand so tenderly and kissed it and said, "Maybe it was for the best." She pulled her hand away and turned her face to the wall. Inside her, a different kind of implantation took place, and the seed of bitterness grew.

IRIS MOVED TO MASON, MISSOURI, two months ago. She didn't want to be in Boston any longer, never mind that her consignment clothes shop had taken off and was flourishing. She didn't want to be in the same town where her happily remarried husband lived.

She ran into Ed and Kathleen at the Museum of Fine Arts. She ran into them at Giacomo's in the North End. After she ran into them at the West Newton Cinema and saw that Kathleen's coat couldn't close over her pregnant stomach, Iris decided to move to San Francisco. She'd always loved the city, and it was time to try something new.

She sold her store, sold her condo and all her furniture, overpacked her SUV with clothes, artwork, and kitchenware, and headed west. But something happened on the way, which was that she got tired of driving, and also she remembered something. She didn't like big cities. She didn't even like medium-size cities. What she liked were small towns, or at least the idea of them.

Someone she'd gone to Boston College with, a girl named Susan Sloat, was from Mason, Missouri. Whenever Susan described it, it was as justification for her never going back, but Iris always liked the sound of it: one river, one cemetery, one department store, with wooden floors and a ribbon department. When the Olive Garden came to town, there was much excitement and a big write-up in the paper; whenever there was a speaker at the library, nearly everyone in town came or had a good reason why they couldn't. Pancake breakfasts, spaghetti dinners, father-daughter dance night: all that her roommate derided, Iris found charming. She thought that living in a small town would be a refreshing change from the Boston suburbs, where she'd been born and raised.

And so it was that on her trip west, she abandoned the idea of San Francisco and drove instead to Mason, Missouri, and settled in. And she was right about the town being a good fit for her. Her only regret about being here is that she didn't come long ago.

She lives in the uppermost corner unit of a three-story brick apartment building, on the banks of the Red Birch River, a narrow, winding waterway into which willow trees dip their branches. In the early morning, she can see mist rising off the water as the

ducks float by, and sometimes at night pieces of moonlight lie on the river like islands. All day, birds flit and
chatter in the trees along the banks. Iris puts breadcrumbs on her kitchen windowsill so that she can
attract them and see them close up, though she
has signed a lease with a provision stating that
she will do no such thing. But everyone does it; in
fact many people affix little feeders to the windows
with suction cups.

Iris bought a guide to the birds of Missouri, and
she has checked off the downy woodpecker, the east-
ern bluebird, the white-breasted nuthatch, the dark-
eyed junco, and the tufted titmouse. She has seen
others, but she doesn't want to check them off yet.
She wants the prospect of more to come. The only
one she doesn't want to see is the mourning dove,
whose name and call press on the bruise.

# Abby

ABBY AND JASON SUMMERS AND THEIR TEN-year-old son, Lincoln, are driving home from Columbia, Missouri, where they've been first to the bookstore and then to Whole Foods. They do this every other Saturday. A good organic grocery store and a bookstore are the only things missing from Mason, as far as they're concerned. Otherwise, they love living here, and have from the first day they moved in. Jason and Abby are both able to work from home, he as a computer consultant, she as a freelance writer for a natural-foods website, and they moved to Mason from Chicago when the congestion in their Wrigleyville neighborhood finally became too much for them. They considered a move to Evanston or Oak Park, but then decided to find a small town they loved. They drove through Mason once on the way to a wedding and had never forgotten how likeable it seemed, and, in fact, is.

But Columbia is a two-hour drive, and going there and back takes up a whole day, mostly because of the way all three of them like to linger in the bookstore. Today is a beautiful mid-October day, but soon the bad weather will be upon them and the drive will take longer.

Abby is exhausted, as she has been for some time. She's exhausted, her gums are bleeding, and last night she found a big bruise on her leg she doesn't remember getting. Today, she stocked up on some herbal medications in Whole Foods that will help. What she minds most is this bone-deep fatigue; she is normally a very energetic person.

She is resting her head against the window, half asleep, when she hears Lincoln say, "I have an idea."

She turns around to smile at him. "What is it?"

"We should open a bookstore in Mason."

"That would be lovely," Abby says. She tightens her coat around her. She's cold all the time lately, too. When she saw her doctor last week, he took some blood from her to find out what's going on. Abby thinks she's probably anemic.

When they get inside the house, Abby says, "I'll make some dinner."

"I got it," Jason says. "You go and rest."

Abby has just taken off her shoes in preparation for lying on the sofa when her cellphone rings. She grabs her purse from the hook by the kitchen door where she has just hung it, pulls out her phone, and answers it.

Jason is chopping carrots for salad and the noise is loud. She goes back into the living room to take the call. It's her doctor, telling her that he needs to speak with her. Can she and Jason come in?

"It's bad news, isn't it?" she says. And then, "Please tell me now. My husband is here. And I want to be home when you tell me."

The doctor hesitates. "It's our normal procedure to have you come in."

"Please," she says.

After she agrees to come to the office the next day, he tells her. She sits for a moment on the edge of the sofa and then she goes back into the kitchen. "Where's Linky?" she asks Jason.

"Up in his room. On his computer, no doubt. He hasn't used up his hour of free time yet. Why?"

Abby moves to stand in front of Jason and wraps her arms around his waist. She says, "Sweetheart. I have leukemia. I have acute myelogenous leukemia." The words are blocky in her mouth. "That's a bad one."

"Abby," he says. He closes his eyes, and together they sway. For one moment, she feels that if she can just stay here, nothing will happen.

# Polly's Henhouse

———

IN THE APARTMENT DOWN THE HALL FROM IRIS lives a taxicab driver named Tiny Dawson, who is the furthest thing from tiny she has ever seen. The man is very tall and is padded with quite a few extra pounds. But he is an extremely kind person—he carried all of Iris's boxes when she moved in, and when Iris protested that he was doing too much, he told her he was in better shape than he looked. He has a friend named Dan, who's the same size or bigger. They go out to eat on Wednesday nights, and Iris often sees Dan climbing into Tiny's truck. There's something touching about it, she thinks, those two big heads inclined fraternally as they go out to wherever they go. She wishes they'd invite her to come along.

One morning about a week after she moved in, Tiny did invite her to have breakfast with him at

Polly's Henhouse. Iris ordered an egg-white omelet with spinach and feta cheese, and whole-wheat toast. Tiny didn't have to order; the buxom waitress brought him a double-size platter of pigs in a blanket, his usual, apparently. He shrugged at Iris after the waitress put the platter down before him. "I guess **I'm** the pig," he said, and Iris said, "I don't think you're a pig, I think you're a very nice man."

"With a weight problem."

Iris began cutting her omelet into small, neat squares. "It's mostly a problem if it bothers you."

"Then it's a problem. I can't quite figure out how to fix it. Nothing I've tried so far has worked."

"I might have a problem like that," Iris said.

"You're not fat!"

"It's not weight. Not that kind of weight, anyway."

Tiny crossed his arms and regarded her. "How old are you, if you don't mind my asking?"

"Forty-seven."

"That ain't old."

**My age isn't my problem,** Iris thought. But she was glad to change the subject, even though she had already sensed that Tiny would be a most empathetic listener, whatever the subject. He had kind eyes, and such a gentle demeanor. He had a way of offering encouragement without saying a word.

"How old are you?" she asked him.

"How old do you think?"

Iris studied him. "Thirty-nine?"

"Damn!"

"Are you thirty-nine?"

"Exactamente."

"Well!" she said, pleased.

Tiny leaned back against the bench of the booth where they sat. "You wouldn't think it to look at me," he said, "but I've dated me a lot of women. A lot of different types and a lot of different ages. Your age? That's the best age."

"Yes, all right," Iris said. "Thank you."

"When you told me your age, you were thinking it was old, right?"

She said nothing.

"Well, it ain't. Not by a long shot. I'll tell you what's old, and this is the God's truth. You ready? Here it is: ninety-three. That's it. You hit ninety-three, and you're old. And that's when you can start smoking. 'Cause it ain't going to kill you before you're dead anyway."

When Iris got home that day, she took off her jacket, and along with it came all the bonhomie she'd just experienced. She stood still in the living room for a while, then went to the desk in her bedroom and pulled out the quietly elegant stationery she'd bought specifically for this purpose. She drew in a breath and began to write. After she finished the letter, she read it, made a few corrections, and read it again. Then she ripped it up and threw it away. A shame, really, the way the heavy cream-colored page with a gold embossed hummingbird at the top now lay in ragged pieces, mixed in with orange peels and bill envelopes.

This morning, Iris lies in bed for a while, watching

the light come to her window. When the rose colors have given over to a whitish yellow, she gets up and showers, dresses in a pair of jeans and a high-necked, pumpkin-colored sweater. Everything's pumpkin now. Clothes, lotions, tea breads, ravioli. People complain about it, but Iris likes it. She's all for celebrating everything. She's grateful to the people who leave Christmas lights up well into February, who bedeck their front porches with flags for the Fourth, with ghosts for Halloween. She likes glittering hearts for Valentine's Day plastered on windows and doors, and blown-out eggs dyed pale pastel colors hanging from trees at Easter time. Never mind that she seems to be an elegant and sophisticated woman, a well-dressed blonde with a Boston reserve and awfully good grammar. At heart, she's a rank sentimentalist.

She makes her bed, looks at her watch, puts on the (pumpkin) coffee, and goes down to the lobby of the apartment building to see if the weekly local paper has arrived. A cat, she's thinking. A dog? And it's time: a job. She has to start meeting more people and adding structure to her days. Nobody looks for jobs in the paper anymore. But in small towns, they do.

Iris pulls out a copy of **Our Town Crier** from the middle of the pile that has been left on the lobby bench. Then she stands by the elevator to go back upstairs. She pushes the elevator button twice, then again, though she knows that does no good at all.

Generally, she likes using stairs in place of elevators anyway, but when she used the stairs here yesterday, there was a wolf spider on the banister that seemed to be poised to jump on her. It had a distressing body size of a good inch and a quarter and it seemed to Iris that all eight of its eyes were focused on her. She was bitten by a spider as a little girl: a trip to the ER, a shot, and nightmares that still crop up every now and then featuring giant arachnids. Iris is an animal lover, but spiders and centipedes don't make the cut.

The elevator door opens and there is Tiny with his magnificent-size (which is to say extra-large) lunch box in hand, apparently off to work.

"Hey, Tiny," she says.

"Hey."

Normally when she sees Tiny, he lights up and chats amiably; his schedule, after all, is his own. But today something is wrong. He won't look at her, and his expression is deeply sad.

"There's a really big wolf spider in the stairwell," she tells him, then immediately regrets it. Is that supposed to cheer him up?

His eyes widen. "Now?"

"I saw it yesterday on the banister at the bottom of the stairwell. It's really big."

"Bigger than a breadbox?"

She smiles. "Just about."

He puts his lunch box down on the bench by the lobby door, then turns to her.

"Watch my lunch. Unless you want to help me kill it."

"Oh, don't kill it!"

"Why'd you tell me about it, then?"

"I don't know. You looked like you could use a little conversation. It was all I could come up with."

"Yeah, I'm having a bad day. Guess it's obvious, huh?"

"We all get them."

"Guess so." He draws in a breath and strides purposefully toward the stairwell.

"Don't kill it!"

"I ain't **going** to kill it. I'm going to capture it and put it in your apartment." He looks over his shoulder at her. "I'm kidding. Come on, watch me get it."

"You know what? I'll wait out here. I'll get the door for you so you can let it go. But take it far from the building. Take it over by the river. Don't let it go in the parking lot. It might get run over. Take it by the river but not too close to the water."

"You're an interesting woman, Iris," he says, and disappears into the stairwell.

Iris sits waiting, thinking maybe this is not such a good idea. Maybe he'll get bitten. And it will be all her fault.

Moments later, Tiny emerges from the stairwell with his hands cupped. "Got it!" He moves toward a trepidatious Iris, and when he is before her, opens up a narrow slit in this hands. There the spider is, frozen in place.

"Ick," Iris says.

"I'll let him go, and then do you want to go and get some breakfast at the Henhouse?"

"Yes!"

"Doesn't the very word make you happy? **Breakfast?** Always does me. That and a rooster on a menu. Give me a rooster on a menu and I'm going to sit right down and order."

"Don't you think you should put that spider out before he bites you?"

"Spider bite ain't going to hurt you none! But hold up here a minute and then meet me at my truck."

"I'll drive," Iris says. "You drove last time."

"Nah, I'll drive," Tiny says, and when Iris starts to protest, he says, "I can't **fit** in your car."

It's an SUV, Iris thinks, but all right.

She finds the classified section in the little paper. There are seven listings under HELP WANTED, all of them for part-time positions, and two could actually work for her. One is for a childcare assistant at Building Blocks Daycare Center for weekends, 3 P.M. to 8 P.M., and the other is for general help for an unnamed small home business, 9 A.M. to noon, Monday through Friday. Iris has always thought it would be more satisfying to have two part-time jobs rather than one full-time one. So she'll apply to both. The salary won't be much for either job, she's certain, but she has enough money to last a long time. For the rest of her life, actually, considering the savvy investments she and her husband made, half of which she was entitled to, and took, on the advice of her formidable female lawyer. Iris didn't want to take anything. But her lawyer said, "Please. Don't be ridiculous." So Iris is set. Financially, anyway. But she thinks a woman her age should work. She thinks she should, anyway. She has to make one last quick trip to Boston to tie up some loose ends with the woman who bought her store, and then she's free.

She stands when she sees Tiny running—well, kind of running, running as best he can—toward her, furiously shaking his hand. "Little fucker bit me!" he says, when she runs out to meet him.

"Oh, no! So did you kill him?"

"No, I didn't kill him! I set him down and he went tearing off into the woods!"

And now, although Iris is not an unsympathetic person, she bursts out laughing. So does Tiny.

"Shall I take you to the ER?" Iris asks.

"The ER!"

"Yes!"

"What are **they** going to do?"

"Treat you for a spider bite?"

"The hell they will. First we'll sit in the waiting room for a day and a half. Then they'll weigh me and try to keep a straight face and then they'll do an EKG and blood work so they can ogle my cholesterol and whatnot. A spider bite will be the least of their concerns. They won't even **get** to a spider bite. No, I ain't going to the ER. I'm going out to breakfast."

"Let me see the bite," Iris says, as though she would have any knowledge about whether or not Tiny needed treatment. But when he shows her his hand, she sees nothing.

"Doesn't look **too** bad," she says. "Let's go and eat. Guess what. I'm getting pigs in a blanket."

"I'm getting the spider-bite special."

"What's that?"

"That's where you get whatever you want on account of some asshole bit you."

In the truck on the way to the restaurant, Tiny says, "Know why I'm having a blue day? Woman trouble. I got a bad crush on one of the waitresses at the Henhouse and I just can't seem to . . . I can't get going with her. Dan says it's because I'm a pushover. He says you have to play hard to get. But it's hard to play hard to get if someone isn't trying to get you. And I don't think Monica is."

"Is she the one who waited on us last time?"

"Nah. She wasn't there last time. She's got long black hair, dimples, gorgeous skin. She's really friendly and she's got a beautiful smile."

"No wonder you're in love with her." Iris watches a bird fly from a tree, and it reminds her that she's meant to ask him something. "Hey, Tiny, I'm wondering if you could do me a favor. I'm going to Boston this weekend for a quick visit, I'll just be gone for a couple of days. I put food out on the kitchen windowsill for the birds every morning and I don't want them to think I've forgotten about them. I don't want them to stop coming."

Funny how important those birds have become to her. But people need something to depend on. They need something to love.

# Monica

—

MONICA MAYHEW BELIEVES THAT A MAN'S disposition can be broadcast by the tilt of his hat. At least she believes that about Roberto Hernandez. The short-order cook at Polly's Henhouse wears a paper hat jauntily at the back of his head when he's in a good mood, and as far down on his forehead as he can get it when his spirit is dark. Today, when Monica comes into the kitchen, she sees that Roberto's hat is nearly obscuring his eyes, and he stares fiercely at the hash browns and onions, his hands on his hips.

"Roberto," Monica says, "give me a cup of oatmeal, will you? I'm going to take my break while it's quiet out there."

"We're out."

"What do you mean we're out?"

"What do you think I mean? It's gone."

"Can't you make more?"

He doesn't answer, just scrapes away some burned bits into the grease trap.

"Roberto?"

He turns around. "You got to have oatmeal? You can't have cold cereal?"

"I don't like cold cereal."

"You don't like it, so I have to make more oatmeal that no one else will eat. We are done with oatmeal for the day. I know these things. Oatmeal stops at eight. Every day. No one wants oatmeal after eight."

Monica knows for a fact that this is not true. But there's no point in provoking him further. He's normally a happy man; she'll forgive him this unpleasantness and just eat a couple of slices of bacon. She reaches for them, and he slaps her hand lightly.

"What?" she says. "I can't have bacon, either?"

"We're running low. See?"

Monica looks at the big pile of bacon Roberto is pointing to. He really is in a bad mood. She grabs three slices.

Roberto puffs air out of his cheeks.

"What's wrong, Roberto?"

He makes a wide gesture toward her shoulder with his long-handled spatula. It looks as though she's being threatened or oddly knighted.

"You don't know what's happening in my house."

Monica waits.

"With my wife. And don't even ask. ¡**Humillante!** That a loyal man has to endure such a thing! I pray for it to be over soon." He kisses his crucifix, flips a row of pancakes. "Don't even ask me!" he says.

Monica doesn't. She chews her bacon.

"All right!" he says. "I will tell you. My wife has these little figures, worry dolls, she calls them. She keeps them in a box, but last week, she takes them out. What are you worried about, I ask her. Nothing, she says. Then why do you have the worry dolls out? I ask. I ask her nice. She don't answer. I get nothing. But I hear from my neighbor Carlos. After I go to work the other day, she is putting on lipstick and swinging her hips for other men. Out she goes to Costco, and she pushes her cart like she is selling herself."

"Roberto, that can't be true."

"Carlos saw. He is sitting at the café having his hot dog and there she goes down the aisle, like in a parade. All made up, her rhinestone clip in her hair. Who do you think bought her that clip?" He jabs his finger in his chest. "Me! I bought it!"

"Maybe she just needed to get a little dressed up and go out."

"To **Costco**?"

"Sometimes a woman just needs to get out of the house. My mom used to go to the five-and-dime and talk to the parakeets. She got dressed up to do it, too. Hose and heels."

"Then your mom, she was a lonely woman who didn't have no love."

Monica waits a careful beat, then says, "Is it possible that Lollie is feeling neglected?"

Roberto snorts. "No way. Every night, I am a bull. You know what I mean. And believe me, she appreciates. But lately, no. She don't laugh, she don't talk much. So you know what? Today, I take those dolls with me. I have them right here in my apron pocket."

Monica sees it now, the little bulge. "What are you going to do with them? You're not going to throw them away, are you?"

He futzes with the onions, mixes them into the hash browns, lays down some French toast.

"She says those dolls hear her. She says they help. So maybe I will talk to them. I will tell them, 'I am worried about my wife. I am worried she will leave me and my children will weep. I am worried she is talking behind my back. I am worried she is in love with another man.' All these little dolls, I give them **my** worries, and then we will see."

Monica says. "You know what I think, Roberto? I think the solution to this is really simple."

He looks at her. "What is it, then?"

"When was the last time you and Lollie had a date?"

He snorts. "Date! Before you marry, you date, then you marry, you no have to date no more."

"Oh, but you do! Lots of married couples schedule date nights."

"Why?"

"Because you have to. . . . It's to keep the love alive. Okay? It's to give your woman something to dress up for. Something to look forward to."

"I take her on vacation once a year. She picks the place, God help us. Also every year, I take her to see her relatives, her big fat mother who breathes fire out her mouth, her father like a shriveled sardine, her old aunt who likes to put her hand on my leg."

"Oh, come on, take Lollie to a pretty little French restaurant."

He makes a face.

"Take her to another kind of restaurant, then. Something with candles. Music. Buy her a fancy drink. Dance. Make conversation."

"We are together every day. You think we don't have conversation when we are together every day?"

"Ask her what she thinks of something. Then listen to what she says. Tell her three things you still really love about her."

"She knows what I still love about her."

"Does she?"

"Maybe you think you can open a clinic for the broken hearts. But I think maybe you are giving advice when you don't know nothing. No offense."

None taken. He's right. She's not married. She doesn't even have a boyfriend. Well, she has a boyfriend, but he doesn't exactly know he's her boy-friend.

She loads two cups of coffee onto her tray and goes back out into the dining room.

"Monica, look!" Polly says, grabbing Monica by the arm and in the process nearly spilling the coffee.

"**Careful!**" Monica says, and looks out the window of the Henhouse to see what Polly's pointing at: Tiny's truck, pulling into the lot.

"It's him!" Monica says.

"What'd I just say!" Polly snatches the tray from Monica. "Here, I'll deliver this, you go and fix your makeup."

"What's wrong with it?"

Polly squints at her. "You'll see. Who ordered the coffee?"

"Teenage couple over in the corner booth," Monica says. "Probably skipping school."

"You can be judge and jury later," Polly says. "Hurry and fix your face and then go and wait on Tiny. And as I keep telling you, give him a sign! Let him know! I don't know where your confidence goes when you fall for a man." Then, looking out the window and drawing back a bit. "Damn. He's got **her** with him again."

"Who?" Monica asks.

"Don't know her name," Polly says. "He brought her in here that day you went to the dentist. Janelle waited on them and got no information whatsoever. Remind me to fire Janelle from my surveillance team."

Monica says nothing, watching Tiny walk into the Henhouse with the woman. She's blond, tall, very pretty, real good posture. Real expensive purse. She's wearing a black cape draped over herself like a model in a magazine. It might be cashmere. She's not from here, that's for sure.

Well, this is a bit unsettling. She's never seen Tiny come in here with another woman, only with Dan. But that woman? Obviously just a friend; now that she's closer, Monica can see she's old enough to be his mother.

In the bathroom, Monica gargles with mouth-wash, freshens her lipstick, pulls off the mascara clots in her lashes. She puts on more blush, then takes it off. Standing back from the mirror, she hikes up her bra straps, checks to see that the bows in her shoe-laces and apron ties are even. Then she yanks the door open to go out.

"Mommy!" a little girl right outside the door says, grabbing her mother's leg.

"Oh, I'm sorry, sweetheart, did I startle you?" Monica asks.

"She's all right," the mother says of her wide-eyed daughter.

"I'm sorry," Monica repeats.

She bends down to speak to the little girl, who hides behind her mother and begins to wail.

**This is a bad sign**, Monica thinks. **It's a bad sign.**

Tiny is in his usual chair at his usual table by the window, and seems deeply engaged in conversation with the woman. He stops talking when Monica comes over, order pad in hand.

"Hey, Monica, good morning!"

"How are you, Tiny?"

He nods, his usual response. Then he points to the woman he's with. "Monica, meet Iris. She lives in my apartment building, just moved in a month ago."

"Two, actually," Iris says, laughing.

She has a low voice, Monica notices. A low, kind of scratchy voice that some might think is sexy, like a singer. Or cute. Or maybe she's got a cold.

Monica herself has a little-girl voice that she despairs of, but what can you do. In her brief sexual history, she has never said things during the Act, despite having heard that it helps. Helps what, she isn't certain, but everyone says you should talk during sex. If she did, though, it wouldn't be in some sultry tone, but rather something that would sound like those dolls you pull a string to make talk.

"I'm having the usual," Tiny says.

"You know, Tiny, we have something new, starting today," Monica says. "You might want to switch it up a bit." And then, she has no idea why she does this, she is not in **cahoots** with this stranger, but she winks at her! And Iris just stares and Monica is instantly humiliated. Why did she **do** that?

But never mind, Tiny is asking what the new thing is.

"Well, it's overnight French toast, and I mean to tell you, it is delicious."

He frowns, considering.

"It makes its own syrup sauce while it cooks and it comes with that thick kind of smoked bacon. It's been real popular, folks just love it. You want to try it?"

"Nah, I'll have the double order of pigs in a blanket, same as always," Tiny says, and right afterward,

Iris says, "Me, too. Although a single order will be fine."

"Coffee?" Monica asks Iris, not smiling and certainly not winking.

"Yes, thank you. Black."

"I know what **you** want," she tells Tiny. "Two hazelnut creamers."

"Right."

"I got you," Monica says. "Be right back." She smiles brightly, and her lips stick to her teeth and she has to turn around to unstick them.

Still. **I know what** you **want. I got you.** That was good. For months, Polly has been saying, "You have got to stop waiting for him to make the first move. Tiny's not like other men. He's not going to figure out you care for him unless you tell him. Or show him. Or something!!"

Well, now Monica has done something.

"Two orders of tucked-in oinkers!" Monica tells Roberto, sticking her head through the little order window. "Make one double-size for Tiny."

"Three oinks," Roberto says. And then, "Hey, Monica. I called my wife. Tonight, dinner out at Mario's and then a movie. She was happy like a little girl. Maybe you were right."

"Maybe I was."

Monica goes over to the register to tell Polly what she said to Tiny, then amplifies it by licking her finger, putting it to her bottom, and making a sizzle sound.

Polly sighs. "That was nothing! For crying out loud, get over there and do something bold. Ask him out!" She unwraps one of the York Peppermint Patties from the little glass dish next to the toothpick dispenser and pops it into her mouth.

Monica blanches. It's hard to tell with her pale skin—she looks like a plus-size Snow White with her black, black hair and her white, white skin. But she blanches.

"My mama didn't raise me like that. I can't ask what the **man** is supposed to ask."

Polly moves in closer. "Modern times paging Monica Mayhew: ask him does he want to go to a movie tomorrow night! It's nothing! Women **propose** to men these days! 'Sides that, there's that app Tinderfire where all you do is say I want to have sex with you. And women go on there the same as men." She pauses, then adds, "I don't **condone** it, but they all do it just the same."

"It's called Tinder," Monica says, "and I would never do such a trashy thing!"

"I'm not saying for you to go on Tinder. I'm saying other women do. And if they can do that, you can ask a guy out for a simple regular date!"

Monica grits her teeth and speaks in a low voice. "Tomorrow night is Saturday night, Polly. That's the big one. I can't start off with Saturday night!"

They turn together toward the sudden sound of loud laughter. It's Iris, and Tiny is sitting with his head down, laughing, too, although silently. That's how he does it, when he laughs, nothing comes out. It's another thing Monica likes about him.

Polly raises an eyebrow.

"All right!" Monica says. "I'll do it."

"Just say—" Polly starts, and Monica says irritably, "I know what to say!" but she doesn't.

When Iris and Tiny's order is ready, Monica brings it to their table. Then, looking just to the left of Tiny, Monica says, "Hey, Tiny, I was wondering . . . would you ever want to go to a movie? Maybe tomorrow night?"

Tiny stops chewing, says nothing.

Monica is going to quit. She's going to throw her apron in Polly's face and quit. She just got a sign not to do this, clear as day, and she ignored it. Now she has embarrassed herself in front of Tiny and that woman. Now he knows she likes him and she can never wait on him again without feeling a fool.

"Wow," Tiny says, finally, and Monica says, "Never mind. It's okay. You need a top-off on that coffee?"

"I . . . gosh, Monica. I'd really like to go to the movie. But I can't go tomorrow. But I don't know, maybe . . ."

"Forget it," Monica says. "It was just . . . you know. It was just a thought."

Yup, she's going to quit. She's going to quit and move to New Orleans. Right after her praline cupcake class tomorrow morning at Lucille Howard's house. Lucille is a genius. Monica even learned how to make Parker House rolls with her, which she always wanted to do. She's not missing that cupcake class, and she'd really like to take the upside-down chocolate pudding cake one, too. So maybe she'll quit the Henhouse but not move. She'll just take a trip to New Orleans. She'll go tomorrow. But . . . alone? She doesn't want to go alone.

When Monica comes back to place another order, Polly leaves the register to come over to her. "How'd it go?"

"He said no," Monica says, and then, through the window to Roberto, "High stack with extra blue, and two staring up!" She turns to Polly. "I quit. I'll finish my shift, but then I quit. I mean it."

"No you don't."

Polly looks over at Tiny. "That son of a bitch."

"Do you want to drive to New Orleans with me this weekend?" Monica asks her.

Polly's mouth drops. "For real?"

"Yep. I've always wanted to go, and I never have."

"Yeah, well. You've never been anywhere." She jabs her glasses up higher on her nose.

"I know that."

"I mean **any**where."

"I **know**. But now I'm going to New Orleans. Do you want to go with me or not?"

"Hell, yes, I'll go. Only we'll fly. I'll treat you."

"No, I can't—"

"We both know Mike left me money. Let me treat you. We'll leave Janelle in charge. She can't do that much damage in a weekend."

Both women regard the skinny waitress laughing with a customer at the counter, she with her throwback beehive and puffed-out bangs. Nothing's wrong with Janelle's heart, in fact she's overly good-hearted and trusting, which is why Polly keeps Janelle's money for her in a cigar box in the office. Janelle can come and take money from it whenever she wants; her no-good lout of a husband can't. It used to be that Janelle's paycheck disappeared hours after she got home; now she actually has an IRA. (The day Polly offered to help her set it up, Janelle said, "But wouldn't my money be in Ireland, then?")

She can be dim, but the customers adore her, the way she calls a group "youse guys," the way she really cares if they like their food, the way she'll take a crying baby and sit with it at the waitress table so the parents can eat.

"Call Suzanne Baxter and see if she wants to work a couple shifts," Monica says. "She misses it here. She can do the cash register and then Janelle won't be nervous about making change."

"That's a good idea," Polly says. "I told Suzanne not to retire; I told her she'd be sitting on her duff all day bored out of her mind and she said, 'Oh, no, I'll be fine.' Well. Every time I see her all she can do is talk about the Henhouse. It's like working here was her glory days. So I'm sure she'll say yes. That stupid Lars will probably be here the whole time she's working; she told me he's gotten so used to her being at his beck and call. But I don't care, let him come, I won't be here for him to annoy with his bad jokes that never even made any sense. This trip is a real good idea, Monica. Mike and I loved New Orleans!"

"And you're sure you want to go again?"

"Oh, hon," Polly says, "you can never get enough of New Orleans." She heads back to the register, and Monica looks over at Tiny just as he looks over at her, and then they both quickly look away.

Never mind. He likes her. She can tell. She may not be very experienced in the world of men, but she's got a good head on her shoulders. Her mama certainly told her that often enough; she'd say, **Neb mind, you've got a good head on your shoulders.** Sometimes Monica wondered if her mama told her that because she was worried about her. Her mama was from a time when young women got married around twenty or so, or they were called old maids. She didn't want Monica to be an old maid. A few days before she died, from her hospital bed, she told Monica, "You find someone, now. Promise me." And Monica said, "I promise. I even have someone in mind."

Her mother held up a trembling hand. "Don't say his name!"

"I know," Monica said. That would be a jinx, her mother thought. Don't say the name of the one you want before you get him. Wear your clothes inside out for good luck. Plant your pole beans by moonlight. Put a penny in your bra when you're asking for a raise.

"Just as soon as you die, I'm going to run right

over and get things going with him good," Monica said, and her mother laughed. That's how they were, the two of them.

"Old maid" is a term that is never used anymore. It's an insult to women, who are stronger and more independent than they ever were. And they're starting to get credit for their worth, now, emphasis on **starting** to, still such a long way to go, including in Monica's own heart and mind and soul. For there is a little place in Monica that will not go away. It is a dark place, over there by her liver, and sometimes it says, **You will never find a man. You** are **an old maid.**

# Strange Goings-On

———

Lucille sits at her kitchen table with a cup of coffee, staring straight ahead and seeing nothing. What a dream she had last night! Not about Frank. Not about Arthur. Not about anything she's ever dreamed of or imagined. She almost can't believe it didn't really happen. But of course it didn't.

In the dream, she was awakened from sleep by the sound of a great thud coming from the backyard. At first, she thought it was an earthquake, and she lay still, trying to remember what she was supposed to do. Stand under a doorframe? But then, moving in the kind of slow-motion, underwaterish manner common to dreams, she went to the window, looked out, and saw a luminescence coming from the bank of hydrangeas running along her back fence.

She cupped her hands around her eyes to see better into the darkness. A figure lay on his side next to the bushes, a man slight in build, short in stature, wearing blue jeans and a T-shirt. She widened her eyes, stepped back, then looked out again. He had something. . . . What **was** that? It looked like he had something growing out of his back.

She put on her robe and went downstairs and out onto her little back porch. "Hello?" she called out.

"Oh! Hello," the man called back.

"Do you need help?"

"Little tangled up here. I can't seem to get up and stay up."

"I'll call the paramedics," Lucille said. "It won't take them long."

"Don't bother. They won't be able to see me. I am invisible to everyone but you."

**Okay,** Lucille thought. **A nutcase.** She opened the door to go back inside and call the police.

"Once, you tried to kill yourself, but you didn't really mean it," the man said.

Lucille turned around slowly. It was true. She did try to kill herself, once, after Frank died. But all that happened is that she threw the pills up. And then Arthur came over and helped her, and well . . . here she is.

"Who **are** you?" she called out.

The man tried to get up again, and fell.

"Tell me who you are!" Any fear she might normally have had was muted in the dream, and she walked right over to the man. He looked like someone she knew, but she couldn't think who.

He sat up, put his hands in a prayer position,

and looked up at her. "Lucille Rachel Howard, I am the angel of death, and I have come to take you home."

"Oh, you are not." But she looked again at his back. **Wings?**

"I'm afraid I am. That pain you had in your chest? It's going to come back in a second, and you—"

"Now, you listen to me. I am not ready and I'm not going with you, I'm going back inside my house. And you just . . ." She waved her hand as though swatting away a fly. "You just go on back where you came from because I am **not ready!**"

She started walking, taking short, huffy steps, then spun around quickly. "For one thing, I have not had my miracle!"

The man smiled at her and spread his arms wide. "What do you call this?"

"You're not even real!" Lucille said, and she ran into the house, slammed the door, and went back to bed.

Now she shakes her head to rid herself of the dream, then goes to the stove to pour herself another cup of coffee. Perked coffee. That's the ticket. People don't use percolators anymore and they don't know what they're missing.

She puts a finger to the center of the coffee cake she baked this morning to see if it has cooled enough for cutting. Yes. She cuts a generous slice and places it on a yellow plate that is perfect for morning. Back at the table, she closes her eyes and takes in a deep whiff. Oh, my. Thank the Lord for green pastures, blue skies, and butter that is 83 percent butterfat. The scent of the cake is so rich it makes her shoulders rise up and her hands squeeze into happy fists. This is a cinnamon-nut crumble with a sweet bourbon drizzle, but Lucille just calls it Granny's coffee cake because everybody always likes Granny's this and Granny's that, keeping some outmoded idea of grannies who used to be able to bake. Well, guess what? Most grannies don't even wear aprons anymore.

Angel of death! Someone once told Lucille that dreams manifest desires that you will not otherwise admit to yourself. But she does not want to die. And it is not time for her to die. She's still got work to do.

She takes a bite of coffee cake, and a memory from long ago comes into her head, that of her as a five-year-old girl, coming into the kitchen one morning and finding her mother sitting at the table with coffee cake, just as Lucille is now. She remembers the inflated sense of importance she had, the urgency to share what had happened to her. She said, "A ghost came into my room last night. It was Grandpa."

Her mother turned a bit in her chair to regard Lucille, but said nothing.

"He sat on my bed, at the bottom, and he talked to me."

Silence, but for the clink of the fork against the plate. And then Lucille's mother said, "Get dressed. You'll be late for school."

"Don't you want to know what he said?"

"You mustn't indulge in such things, Lucille. And you must not speak of them to others."

Now Lucille rises slowly out of her chair to look over the half-curtain into the backyard. Nothing.

# The Future Foretold

MONICA IS AT THE HOUSE OF RISING VISIONS in what she guesses they would call the lounge, waiting for Polly to come out from the red-velvet-curtained cubicle where she's having her fortune told. Monica finished first, and is kind of excited to tell Polly what she heard, even though she thinks it will probably be essentially the same thing Polly gets told. Monica doesn't really believe in fortune-telling. She believes in signs, but that's information that comes from within herself, from her own unconscious, not from some stranger who takes Visa.

Last night at dinner Polly insisted that a trip to New Orleans was incomplete without a visit to a fortune-teller, and she suggested they go to one before they left for the airport. It surprised Monica that Polly would have such a strong belief in them. But Polly went on and on, talking about how there

**are** ways to divine things, there are people who can intuit things, come on, hadn't Monica ever heard of those psychics who help the police find crime victims and lost items? Hadn't Monica herself ever had a psychic vibe about something?

"No," Monica said. "Nope, I have had signs, but I have never had a psychic vibe."

"You're just saying that because you don't want to go to a reading," Polly said.

"No I'm not! And anyway, I doubt that the people we'd be seeing are real psychics like those cop ones. Plus, it costs too much."

"I'll treat you," Polly said, and she just wouldn't stop, and so, fine, here they are at the fortune-telling Mall of America.

It does seem like a kind of mall, though maybe "strip mall" is more accurate. The place is long and narrow, just a line of six cubicles with fortune-tellers inside, with a row of chairs for people waiting on the other side of the booths. Lots of red and black, lots of velvet, dim lights on some ratty chandeliers. When they first walked in, there was a man who was available, but neither Polly nor Monica wanted him—they asked if they could wait for a woman. "Suit yourself," the man said, and went out for a smoke. Monica thought that was unprofessional. She thought he might have said something like, "I see you have had bad experiences with men."

Monica got a woman who seemed to look the part: long black hair, a great deal of eyeliner, long red fingernails, a throaty voice. She wore a full-length, black velvet dress embroidered in silver thread with all kinds of things, including suns and moons and pentagrams. Her little table was covered with a black silk shawl, and it had the longest fringe Monica had ever seen. She kind of wanted that shawl. If she'd had enough nerve she would have asked to buy it, but she was pretty sure it wasn't for sale.

The fortune-teller, whose name was Twilight (**Sure it is,** Monica thought), had a few different kinds of tarot cards. She had what she called a divining stick, decorated with beautiful stones. She even had a crystal ball, but that was extra if you wanted her to look into it for you. Praying for you after your visit, that was extra, too, but highly recommended. "No thank you," Monica said, a bit too emphatically, perhaps. She requested a basic tarot card reading.

She looks at her watch, crosses her legs, and starts to jiggle her foot. Polly has to come out now, or they're going to miss their flight. She leans forward, straining to hear what's going on, but can't. And then she decides not to try to eavesdrop anyway. It would be wrong, like listening in on someone's confession. Which, actually, she has done and then felt bad about, but who could walk away from a guy confessing pretty loudly about infidelity with his wife's best friend? And he didn't even get that bad a penance, just a couple of rosaries and a promise that he would stop the affair and go to a therapist. Well, maybe the man did. Maybe the wife was a shrew and deserved

to be cheated on. Monica shouldn't be so judgmen-
tal. She shouldn't eat so much bread.

The bell over the door tinkles and two young
women come in, giggling. The man comes out and
says he's available if one of them would like to come
with him. They look at each other and then ask if
they can be seen together.

"Up to you," the man says. "You both have to pay
the full amount. And I'm going to say some real
personal things about y'all in front of each other."

"That's okay," they say, all singsongy and together,
and Monica feels sure they're cheerleaders. Maybe
it's something in the air, but she really does feel sure
they are cheerleaders. Dallas Cowboys cheerleaders.
She feels so sure she wants to ask them, but she
doesn't. "I'm Midnight," the man says, and the girls
say (together), **Ohhhhhhh,** and Monica rolls her
eyes. They disappear behind the curtain.

She is just about to knock on Polly's curtain,
should she be able to do such a thing, when Polly
bursts out of the little space, grinning.

"What did yours say?" Monica asks, as they walk
quickly (a little too quickly, for Monica's taste, but
Polly would move quickly if she were ascending the
ladder to the gallows).

"Wait till we're in the car!" Polly says. "The crystal
ball reading, oh, my God!" Now Monica feels bad
that she didn't get the crystal ball reading, too.

"Did you get the she'll-pray-for-you thing?" she
asks.

"Of course!" Polly says. "Didn't you?"

"No," Monica says. Then, apologetically, "I was too cheap."

"I was paying!" Polly says, and Monica says, "I know." And then she doesn't really want to share what Twilight told her anymore. Because it wasn't even that interesting and it was not what she wanted to hear. She probably should have gotten the crystal ball reading.

As it happens, Monica doesn't have to worry about saying anything, because Polly starts talking a mile a minute and does not let up until they reach the airport. Her psychic told her that she was going to meet a man who would become more of a friend than a lover but he would be a good friend and they would end up living together. He would take her often to Paris, where it looked like he might have an apartment? A permanent hotel room? "And then she looked at me as if I should know," Polly, says, laughing. "So I said, 'An apartment, with a beautifully stocked kitchen.' And then she said, 'Oh, no, he's not a cook. Never has been a cook. That's where you'll come in, because you're a cook, am I right? Your job is something with food.'"

"Wow," Monica manages to fit in.

"Yeah, and she told me that I am going to get a dog, a dachshund, which she knew I have always secretly wanted but never got, but now I will, a red doxie, maybe a mini one."

Oh, it went on and on. That Polly should wear more yellow because it lit up her aura and brought her good fortune. That her business would thrive until she sold it, and then it would go under. "Which actually made me kind of happy, which I guess is small of me," Polly says.

She keeps talking, and Monica gets bored and starts thinking about the food they had there, chickory coffee, red beans and rice—the rice and beans were just from a fast-food stand, and they were so good! They also had oysters Rockefeller at Antoine's, and Monica tried escargots, so fun to even say, and she's going to tell Lucille Howard all about that because Lucille said one day in her baking class that eating snails was one thing she wanted to do. Well, wait till Monica tells her they were **escargots à la bordelaise,** baked in red wine and garlic sauce and sprinkled with cheese and breadcrumbs they made out of French bread. And oh, those muffulettas! They got them from the Central Grocery because Polly said they had to get them there. They thought about sharing one because they were so huge but then they didn't share and they both ate every last bite. Monica told Polly they should put muffulettas on the menu at the Henhouse and Polly said it would be too hard to find the right olive salad to put on top and Monica said you could get everything on the Internet now. "Who would eat them, though, in Mason?" Polly asked, and Monica said, "Us! And Tiny!"

"Yeah, Tiny'll eat purt near everything," Polly said.

That was true, except at breakfast, when he refused to eat anything but the same thing he always had.

At the gate, Polly asks Monica what her fortune-teller said.

"Oh, not so much, really," Monica says. "She knew my dad had died when I was real young. She said my mom was watching from heaven. She said I was going to get married soon, but to a man whose first name starts with **P**."

"**P**?" Polly says. "Are you sure she said **P**? **P** sounds a lot like **T**, you know."

"I'm sure. I even said, 'You mean **P** like **Paul**,' and she said, 'Yes, but it isn't Paul. Or Peter.' She might be wrong," Monica adds.

"I suppose," Polly says, but Monica can tell she doesn't think so.

"Huh," Polly says.

They fall asleep on the plane just like that because one thing about New Orleans is you don't sleep much because of the beckoning fingers of jazz and zydeco music and the meandering crowds holding great big glasses of booze and the bright-colored beads and the whoo-ha and yee-ows as people spin wildly around on dance floors and the exotic-looking drag queens (the only people who can wear blue eyeshadow and wear it well) and the Creole you hear and all the other languages and the horses and buggies and gaslights and even the danger, even the little sense of danger they felt when they were followed back to their hotel a bit too closely by a couple of really seedy-looking characters. Well, seedy in New Orleans is romantic. Everything there is romantic. When she marries P., she's coming to New Orleans on her honeymoon. She hopes T. will be good and sorry.

# Step One

===

J ASON AND ABBY ARE WAITING AT THE HOSPITAL in a little room where Abby will soon receive her first chemotherapy treatment. She's brought her own pillow and she is lying under the compass quilt her mother made and just sent her, all purples and blues, healing colors. **You will find your way,** the note her mother included said. Just now, just for a moment, Jason wonders if Abby wishes she had taken her mother up on her offer to come stay with them. But her mother suffers from health problems herself—severe arthritis, occasional atrial fibrillation—and Abby didn't want to tax her any more than the news of her daughter's diagnosis already had.

Abby's mother, Joan, was on speakerphone when they called to give her the news, and they looked at each other when the first thing Joan said was, "I'm coming. I'll get the first flight out. I'll take a taxi to your house."

"Thank you, Mom, but maybe it would be good to save you for later on," Abby said, and her mother said, "Are you sure?"

"It's just that we're taking in a lot right now. Trying to figure things out. Jason and I, I mean. Linky doesn't know yet. It'll be hard, telling him."

"He might get mad at you," Abby's mother said.

"Yes, I've read that. Because of his fear, he might lash out at me. And at Jason. His schoolwork might suffer. That's why we haven't told him yet. And anyway, I'm feeling okay right now. So we'll wait on having you come. Okay?"

"All right. Whatever you want. But I'm here, honey."

"I know." Abby pressed two fingers to her mouth, rocked back and forth.

"Call if you need me for anything. Or if you want to talk. Call anytime, night or day."

"I will."

After they hung up, Abby wept in Jason's arms.

Now she looks into his eyes and whispers, "I'm so scared."

He takes her hand and rubs it between his own. Kisses it.

"Are **you** scared?" she asks.

He shakes his head no, but doesn't look at her.

"Jason?"

"I'm a little scared," he says, "but I also know you're going to be fine."

"How do you know?"

"I just do."

She smiles. "No you don't."

He is about to argue when the nurse comes up to start the IV. But first she confirms identification, asks about any allergies, and so forth. Jason feels a sudden fullness in his bladder and points to the nearby bathroom. Abby nods, then tells the nurse, "I got a rash with amoxicillin once."

It comes to Jason that so many things that get said now seem . . . well, they seem ridiculous. Surreal. Beside the Big Point. Yet life goes on, it must go on, with its small pronouncements and mundane activities, with its unrelenting necessities. The evening after they got the news, Abby came out of the bathroom, saying, "You know, it seems so odd that so much still **works**."

"You mean . . . ?" Jason said, and Abby flopped down beside him on the sofa and said, "I mean, I'm waiting for all the **other** shoes to drop."

Jason looks in the hospital bathroom mirror to practice what he wants to say. "You'll go into remission," he says. "I know you will." Not all that convincing. Well, that's because he's not all that convinced.

"We'll get through this," he tries. Better.

**We'll** get through this. Right. Like **we** were pregnant. Right.

When Lincoln was born, Jason was in attendance the whole time, and he thought, **God, I'm glad** I **don't have to do this.** And he felt guilty about that.

And now? Does he wish it were him going through this rather than her? He wishes he could say yes.

Back at Abby's bedside, he sees the IV in her hand, the time and date written on the white dressing over it. A little smiley face is drawn on there, too.

Jason points to the smiley face and rolls his eyes.

"I know," Abby says. "But she's sweet. God, she's young, too!"

"New grad?"

"I didn't ask her. I was afraid to. I want someone with experience."

Jason looks around the room. "Everybody seems really competent, though."

"Yeah. I guess."

"Do you want anything? Do you want some almonds or something?"

"No thanks."

"Want me to read to you?"

"I don't think I could really listen."

"Well, then, let's just conversate."

She smiles, as she always does when he uses that word. **Conversate.**

"That's not a word" she told him the first time he used it.

"Nothing used to be a word until the first time it got used," he responded.

"You know, you can never take criticism," she told him.

He frowned, thinking. Then he asked, "Is that true?"

"I don't know," she said. "Let's conversate about it."

Now **conversate** is in their own personal clubhouse, along with blueberry oatmeal pancakes and fresh-squeezed orange juice and **The New York Times** every Sunday morning. They talk to their dog, Henry, as though he's another person. They fall asleep on the sofa at night in front of the TV and then they go upstairs to bed and that wakes them up a little and so they read side by side until they fall asleep again. Once, she told him that reading together was better than sex.

"Really?" he asked.

"Well, just as good as," she said. And then, quickly, "Okay, almost as good," and then he was content.

"So what do you think of our neighbor lady?" Jason asks.

"I told you. She's odd, but nice enough."

"But would you trust her with Lincoln?"

"I don't know. Maybe. If we have to. But she'd feed him **sugar**."

"I don't think we can worry about stuff like that now. He did seem to like her well enough."

"Well, yeah. As an oddity."

"No," Jason says. "I think he really liked her. When I went in to see him before bed that night, he said, 'Do you think you could ask Lucille **anything**, and she'd just be **honest**?'"

Abby smiles. "Right. Honest she is, though I'd call it rude. '**Well, I can't say I care for tofu lasagna.**'"

"But she ate it."

"Indeed."

"She's comfortable with kids," Jason says. "She taught for a long time. And she lives right next door. It's handy."

"We'll see," Abby says. "She's awfully old."

"But she's healthy!"

Abby nods and looks down, and Jason wishes he could take back what he said. **She's healthy, as opposed to you.**

Abby looks up at her IV bag, with its garish fluorescent orange label, she looks at her watch, she looks around the room at all the little cubicles with patients like her hidden from view. They hear a long, low groan, and Abby looks at Jason. "Maybe some almonds, after all. Or maybe . . . a Snickers bar? With almonds?"

"You don't eat Snickers bars!"

"Not since I was twenty years old. So yeah, not for twenty years. But you know what? I look at them. Every time I go to the grocery store here, I look at them. Sometimes I squeeze them. They make them now with two in one package. Get that, and then you can have one. We'll see if they're like we remember."

"Want a **National Enquirer,** too? They have them in the gift shop."

"Are you kidding?"

"Would I kid about a thing like that? I'll get you one."

"And a **Star** magazine?"

"If they have it, I'll get it."

He kisses her forehead. He loves her so. Her and
Lincoln and their lazy dog, Henry, and their life
together. Sometimes at night, when she's sleeping,
he lets himself think about what life would be like
without her. At those times, he can hardly breathe.

# Hired or Fired?

===

"I'M SORRY I'M LATE," IRIS SAYS TO LUCILLE, THOUGH three minutes after the appointed hour is not what most people would call late. "The last interview I had took a bit longer than I thought it might."

"You're coming from another job interview?" Lucille asks.

"Yes."

"Where?"

"Building Blocks Daycare?"

"I see. So this is a competition?"

"No, not at all. You're both part-time."

Lucille steps back from the front door. "All right. Well, come on into the kitchen. Can I offer you something? Coffee or tea?"

Iris declines, and sits in the chair that Lucille has pointed to. The walls are covered with children's drawings, and Iris tries very hard not to look at them. Instead, she focuses on a coconut cake at the center of the table, one slice removed to reveal what looks like lemon filling.

"What a beautiful cake!" Iris says.

"You can't have any of that," Lucille says. "That's my demo cake for the class I'm teaching later today. I make a demo for every class I teach. That way, the students are inspired the moment they walk in the door. They see what we're going to do, I give them the recipe, and then they learn how to make it. While the second cake is baking, we have a question-and-answer period, and then, when both cakes are done, we eat them. Most of them go right ahead and try the recipes again at home, right away. They want to show off for their families and friends. And they get all excited because I teach them secrets that not everyone knows." She points to the cake. "For example, in this case? Citric acid in the lemon filling. You **want** that pucker."

"Yes, of course," Iris says, though she's not completely sure what Lucille means. She can cook savory things, but she has never gotten into baking. Ed was one of those rare people who didn't like sweets, and she didn't want to bake for one, so she never learned how.

"For heaven's sake," Lucille says, "look at most of the lemon meringue pies you get when you eat out. First of all, the crust is horrible, that goes without saying. But the filling is usually way too sweet, too. Sweet and gummy and that terrible garish yellow.

What a disappointment to order a slice of a lemon pie and not taste lemon at all!"

"Right!" Iris says.

"Now, you look like a perfectly fine person. Nicely dressed, well spoken, and I'm glad to see you have no visible tattoos. Or body parts pierced where they should not be. But before we go any further, I want to give you a little quiz. Just a little one, a few basic questions. Because it will be the sine qua non. All right?"

**Uh-oh,** Iris thinks, but she says, enthusiastically, "Sure!"

Lucille goes to a kitchen drawer and takes out a piece of paper. "Now. I've got it all prepared, and here are two sharpened number-two pencils, and I'm going to give you fifteen minutes, I don't feel you should need more time than that. I'll leave the room." She puts the test facedown in front of Iris. "You may begin." She starts to leave, then turns around and says, "No cheating!"

She says this last part merrily, as though it's a joke, but Iris doesn't think it is.

After fifteen minutes, Lucille peeks her head into the kitchen. "Finished?"

Iris is not; she's holding the pencil over the paper and staring intently down. Her stomach aches. But she was warned that she'd get only fifteen minutes and, looking at her watch, she sees that fifteen minutes are indeed up. "I guess so," she says.

Lucille sails smoothly into the kitchen and stands expectantly before her.

Iris hands her the quiz.

Lucille sits down at the kitchen table. "All right, let's go through the questions together, shall we?" She rearranges her bottom on the chair. "Number one. What is the best way to tell if meringue has been whipped enough?

"**A toothpick,** you say. Well, no. That's wrong. The correct answer is that you turn the bowl upside down. If it's ready, the meringue will stay in the bowl." Using a red pencil, Lucille makes an **X** beside Iris's answer.

"Number two. What is a quick way to bring raw, refrigerated eggs to room temperature? **Microwave,** you say. Huh. Microwave. Now, Irene."

"It's Iris."

"What?"

"It's Iris. My name is Iris."

"Oh, you're right, I beg your pardon. Right. Iris, like the flower. Well, Iris, your answer is not a totally unreasonable answer, but it, too, is wrong. You cannot control the heat enough with a microwave. The right answer is to put the eggs in your bra. Your body temperature will gently warm them in just a few minutes. Okay?"

"Okay," Iris says.

"Number three. What can you add to milk to make it a substitute for buttermilk? You say, **Butter.**" Iris hears a tiny sigh escape Lucille. "This also is wrong. The right answer is to add a bit of vinegar or lemon until the milk curdles."

"Oh. Isn't that interesting!"

Lucille looks over at her in what Iris would call a severe way, and Iris looks down into her lap.

"Number four. If you can't get fresh, which is better, canned or frozen? Well! For this one you said, **Frozen,** and that is correct. Congratulations.

"Number five. Why should pie crust be refrigerated before you roll it out? You say, **Because it's a good place to keep it until you're ready for it.** Oh, my. Wrong. You refrigerate it so that it keeps its shape. Have you ever even rolled out pie crust?"

"You mean the kind in the grocery store?"

Lucille closes her eyes.

"Number six. What is the difference between baking powder and baking soda? You say, **One comes in a can and one comes in a box.**" Oh, Lord. That is true, but it is not the right answer. The answer is that baking powder is a leavener that contains both sodium bicarbonate **and** flavor-saving acid, and so it is usually paired with non-acid ingredients like whole milk and Dutch-processed cocoa. Baking soda **needs** an acid; baking powder already **has** an acid. If you were to try to substitute baking soda for baking powder in a recipe where no acidic ingredient is present, there would be no release of gas and therefore no rising would occur."

"Ah," Iris says.

"Number seven. Should one use orange zest or orange juice when making orange cream cheese spread? You answered, **What is orange cream cheese spread?** And you failed to even try to answer the last three questions."

Lucille lowers Iris's paper onto her lap and looks over her glasses at her.

Iris smiles. Shrugs.

"Do **you** think I should hire you?"

Iris says nothing.

"I must tell you that I had decided beforehand to accept only a certain number of errors in this test. What do you think that number was?"

Iris has no idea. But she says, "Four?"

"Nope. It was zero." Lucille stands. "It was very nice meeting you, Miss Winters. I hope you'll be happy at the daycare center. Let me walk you out."

Iris stays sitting. "You know . . . I can't work there, actually."

"Why not?"

"Because they won't hire me. When I went into the baby room, I started to cry. Because I feel so bad that I never had a baby. And I really wanted one. And now it's too late."

A cuckoo clock on the kitchen wall sounds the hour, and both women fall silent. Eleven times the little door opens and closes and the bird says, "**Cuckoo!**"

And then Lucille speaks quietly. "I never had a baby, either. I'm lucky to have a young woman in my life, Maddy, who is like a daughter to me. She has a little girl named Nola, and I call her my grandchild. Those are Nola's drawings on the wall. But I never even got married. I only got engaged. He died before we could get married."

"I'm so sorry," Iris says, and her eyes fill with tears.

Some of it is for Lucille and some of it is for herself.

"I'm sorry, too," Lucille says, and then, "I hope you can understand, though, that your test results indicate that you would have a very difficult time working here. I need someone who knows what they're doing." She folds Iris's test in half and stands. "I do thank you for coming."

Iris leans forward and speaks earnestly. "Lucille, I can cook, but as you have seen, I'm no baker. Still, I think I can really help you. I ran a very successful business back in Boston. I can make you a website, do spreadsheets, figure out ways to grow your business, and find creative and inexpensive ways to advertise. I can write course descriptions and make it so people can sign up online, and the fees for the classes would be direct-deposited into your bank account. And I am utterly dependable."

Lucille looks at her. "I don't know. . . ."

"Plus I'll work for peanuts. Because I don't need the money, I just want to work. And . . . well, I want you to know that whether you decide to hire me or not, I really appreciated learning what I just did from you. You're a good teacher."

Lucille narrows her eyes. "What's the difference between baking soda and baking powder?"

Lightning-fast, Iris shoots back, "Baking powder has an acid, baking soda needs one."

Lucille stares at her. And then she says, "Oh, all right, you're hired. You can start next Monday. At least you have nice penmanship. You go ahead and do that computer mumbo-jumbo. Also, you can help with setup and cleanup. And you can shop for supplies. But don't even think about interacting directly with the students, I have a reputation to maintain. Deal?"

Iris holds out her hand and Lucille shakes it.

On her way home, Iris thinks about the baby room she'd seen at the daycare center, the cheerful yellow walls, the polka-dotted curtains, the white cribs, the sight of six or seven little ones, some sleeping, some awake, one standing at the side of her crib, holding out her arms to Iris. Nothing could have prepared Iris for the emotional response she had. She didn't start to cry; she started to sob. The director looked at her, alarmed. "I'm sorry," Iris said. "I guess I'm not . . . I'm sorry." And she fled the room.

Thank goodness for Lucille taking a chance on her. She won't let her down.

# Maddy and Nola

—=—

IT IS A SPECTACULARLY BRIGHT SATURDAY MORN-
ing, the kind of day that always makes Lucille feel
as though the sun has been through the car wash. It's
a welcome thing after so many gray days in a row.
She is still in her pajamas, just rinsing out her coffee
cup, when she hears a rapping at the door. Who
could this be, at such an indecent hour? She looks
up at the kitchen clock and sees that it's 10:50. All
right, not such an indecent hour, but still, no call,
no warning of any kind. It's probably one of those
religious people shoving pamphlets at you, smiling
their wide smiles, but with a note of pity in their
eyes for your sorry state—soon to be rectified, if only
you would let them. Lucille used to try to explain
why she wasn't interested, but that never worked, so
one day she tried something different, which was to
pretend she was French and couldn't speak English.

A teacher friend who had taught French at the high school used to give Lucille private lessons now and then, mostly so that Lucille could pronounce the names of French desserts with a certain flair. But wouldn't you know it, the one time Lucille tried to say she didn't speak English—in French, of course—the do-gooder's eyes lit up and she said, **"Ah, vraiment? Mais je parle français!"** Then Lucille had to quickly look ill and say, **"Pardon, pardon, je me sens malade,"** and slam the door. Well, that woman stood there for a full minute before she left a pamphlet in the mailbox, and then she went on to Arthur Moses's house, next door to Lucille's, and didn't Arthur just invite that woman right in.

Arthur was not a religious man, he never went to church and he once told Lucille that he saw God in the eye of a daisy. But he invited that woman in and then she didn't leave for half an hour! Lucille kept an eye out in case Arthur might need help, periodically looking out her kitchen window into his, but of course he didn't. And the woman left smiling after what appeared to be a most amiable chat. That's how Arthur was. You could get all up in arms about this or that, but Arthur would, by quiet example, remind you of the worth of simple kindness no matter what the occasion. It could get on your nerves sometimes.

Now the doorbell rings, and she tightens her robe belt and goes to answer it. She opens the door and before her is . . . no one. But then she hears, "Hi, Grandma Lucille!" and she looks down to see towheaded five-year-old Nola, her hair in pigtails that stick out of the sides of her head like handles. She has a cellophane-wrapped bouquet that she holds up now, saying, "This is for you!" It's a bouquet from the grocery store, so it has those irritating alstroemeria that never die, even when you want them to, but it **is** always the thought. Nola's mother, Maddy, is coming up the walk from the car, dragging a suitcase, a bedraggled teddy bear, and a bag of groceries. "Hi, Lucille!" she says. "Surprise!" It is indeed a surprise, but since it's Maddy, it's fine.

Nola runs past Lucille and into the living room, where she will want to fool around with the music box Lucille's mother gave her, which Lucille keeps on her coffee table. Lucille feels torn about whether to wait for Maddy to come in or to go over and say to Nola, "Now, remember to be **gentle**."

Luckily, Maddy comes rapidly toward her and embraces Lucille, and then Lucille is free to move into the living room, where she sits down on the sofa, an arm's length away from Nola. The little girl is kneeling on the floor in front of the music box, regarding it as though it is a rare Egyptian artifact just now unearthed from the sand. "Wind it?" Nola says, and Lucille does.

The music box is rosewood, with flowers etched on the surface. It plays five songs: "Rio Rita," "Two Hearts in Waltz Time," "Blue Danube," "Donkey Serenade," and "In an Eighteenth-Century Drawing Room." If you lift the lid, you can see through a clear piece of glass how the thing works, the turning cylinder with its tiny pins, the teeth of the steel comb that get plucked like a harp. Lucille had never met anyone as enchanted by the box as she was, but then along came Nola. Lucille has left the music box in her will for the child, but for now, she watches, hawklike, as Nola moves her hand closer to the box. Nola is watching Lucille the same way. "Caaaaareful," Lucille says, and Nola whispers back solemnly, "I knooooow." And then, suddenly sitting back on her heels, "Grandma, do you have some cookies for me?"

**Now you're talking,** Lucille thinks, and though her mother says, "Nola, you wait to be **offered**," she and Nola head hand in hand for the kitchen and the big self-satisfied porcelain pig with his hooves crossed over his belly, Lucille's favorite cookie jar. "You go ahead and take one," Lucille tells Nola, lowering the jar. "They're sugar cookies stuffed with raspberry jam, and I made the jam, too, and is it ever good."

"May I have two?" Nola asks.

"All right," Lucille says, meeting Maddy's eyes. She is leaning against the doorjamb with her arms crossed, smiling and shaking her head. **My,** Lucille thinks, **she's become such a beautiful young woman.** And there's a certain glow that makes Lucille wonder, **Is she pregnant again?**

Then Maddy holds up her left hand. A ring! It's not a diamond, but what appears to be an emerald. Lucille points to it. "Is that what I think it is? Are you engaged?"

Maddy nods happily. "I came to tell you in person."

Lucille has a million questions about who this fellow might be. But there is another question that is preeminent for Lucille: she asks, "Can I make the wedding cake?"

"Of course! I was hoping you would. But can you make it chocolate **and** vanilla?"

Lucille gives her a look.

"Good," Maddy says. "That part's done, then."

"Can I have another cookie?" Nola asks.

"Nope," Maddy says. "We're going to get started on lunch. We're going to make Grandma Lucille lunch and dinner, remember?"

"Yes, and lunch is BLTs and dinner is salad and chicken with some lemons stuffed inside and green rice."

"Green rice?"

Nola nods, and then whispers sloppily into Lucille's ear: "It's **spinach**."

"Did you move the aprons?" Maddy calls from inside the pantry.

"Yes, I keep them in the hall closet, now that there are so many. Got a lot more vintage ones from Time's Treasures. The students in my classes love them."

"I want to see," Maddy says.

Lucille hears Maddy oohing and ahhing over the new additions. She comes back into the kitchen wearing the Eiffel Tower apron with the little French poodles with bows in their hair. That's a popular one. The students seem to think they'll become Julia Child when they wear that apron, even though Lucille doubts most of them can make a decent omelet. But never mind, at least they come dying to learn how to make something special—pecan divinity cake, for example. Cream puffs. Peach cobbler. Raspberry lemonade pie, oh they practically kissed her feet when they learned that one.

"So the classes are going well?" Maddy asks.

"Very well," Lucille says. "In fact I just hired an assistant to help me. She'll start next week. But never mind the classes. Who are you **engaged** to?"

Maddy sits down at the kitchen table opposite Lucille. She folds her hands and leans forward to say, "My professor."

"No!"

"Yes."

"That young and handsome one?"

"No, the other one, the old one. Nineteen years older than I am. And he's not exactly handsome."

"Well," Lucille says, making her tone as diplomatic as possible, "age isn't—"

"I'm kidding!" Maddy says. "It's the young, super-handsome one, the one who sent my work to the magazine and got my pictures published that first time. His name is—"

"His name is Matthew!" Nola says. "Matthew Allbright!"

"Do you like him an awful lot?" Lucille asks, turning to Nola.

"Yes!"

"Are you going to be a flower girl?"

Nola looks at Maddy, who shakes her head no.

"Why isn't she going to be a flower girl?"

"It's going to be a really small wedding. If you're all right with it, I'd love to have it here. There'd only be a few guests."

"Well, of course you can have it here! It's your house. I'm just the tenant."

"Not anymore."

"What do you mean?"

"I had the deed put in your name. It's all yours now."

"Oh, Maddy, that doesn't make any sense!" But then she says, "Well, for heaven's sake. Thank you, Maddy. I guess you won't be moving back here to Mason, then."

"No. In fact, right after I graduate in June, we're moving to New York. To Brooklyn."

"New York!" Lucille looks over at Nola.

"She loves New York," Maddy says. "I hope you'll visit us there. There are a lot of wonderful bakeries doing all kinds of creative things there."

"I suppose that's fine," Lucille says. "If you like that sort of thing."

"Lucille, get dressed," Maddy says. "We'll eat lunch and then find something fun to do. Then we'll come home and Nola and I will make you dinner."

"All right," Lucille says, and heads upstairs. She has no idea what might be fun to do in Mason. They'll need to drive awhile to find some fun. But that's fine, she would actually like a drive, so many of the trees still glorious. There's a cooking store about thirty miles away that she'd love to visit. It's called Good Looking Cooking, and it's run by two sisters, and they have the cutest cookie cutters (Lucille thinks she'll buy the turkey one and the stacking hearts), and they have a lot of beautiful cupcake wrappers—rainbow-colored, polka-dotted, silver and gold, even lace-cut. Someone in Lucille's class put her name on the store's mailing list and they send Lucille their catalog, but of course you need to see things in person. People who do catalogs get paid a lot of money to make things look good. Then when you order them, the store demands credit card information on the phone without so much as a by-your-leave. Why, anyone could take that information and do anything with it! And then when the things finally arrive, half the time they aren't what you thought they'd be. They don't fit. They're made cheaply. They're a different color than they seemed to be. Worst of all is when they don't work, oh, that's the most infuriating, you get it, you try it, nothing! A dud! And then there you go, hauling the thing to the post office when you have far better things to do. No. You need to see things before you buy them. You need to touch them. You need someone in the store who knows what the hell they're talking about when you ask about the merits of this or that. She'll ask Maddy to take her to Good Looking Cooking. Nola will like it, too. She'll let the little girl pick out a cookie cutter. Or two.

Lucille is standing in her bedroom in her underwear when Nola bursts through the door.

Lucille thinks about trying to cover herself, but the damage is done.

"You have big bosums," Nola says.

"I suppose I do. What about it?"

"Nothing. Can I sit on your bed?"

"Yes."

"Can I jump on it?"

"No."

"Okay." She sits on Lucille's bed, then lies on it, and Lucille finishes getting dressed: gray wool slacks, a pink V-neck sweater.

"Do you wear a girdle?" Nola asks.

Lucille sits beside her to put her socks and shoes on. "No, I do not wear a girdle. Not anymore. How do you even know what a girdle is?"

"Mommy told me. She took a picture of some girdles." She puts her hands over her mouth and giggles.

"Whatever for?"

Nola offers an elaborate shrug. Then, seeing Lucille struggle to bend over to tie her shoes, she says, "Want me to do that? I know how to tie."

"Okay."

Nola hops off the bed and tends to the task. "Do you like these shoes?" she asks, of the orthopedic black sneakers Lucille favors.

"Yes, I do."

"Do you think they're pretty?"

"No, but I think they're comfortable. And that's what matters most to me."

Nola slowly ties the second shoe.

"You're doing a good job there, Nola."

"Yes. Thank you. I know—we could get you pink laces. They have sparkle ones."

"Let's look for some today. And, oh, my goodness, I almost forgot. I'm teaching a kids' class tomorrow afternoon. You can come!"

"I can?"

"Of course!"

"Can I wear the star apron?"

"Of course!"

"Can we make Mississippi mud cookies?"

"I'll make those for you while you're here, and you can take them home. But in the class, we're making chocolate-dipped potato-chip cookies."

Nola screws up her face. "**Potato**-chip cookies?"

"They happen to be delicious," Lucille says. "But if you don't think you're interested—"

"I'm interested!" Nola says quickly.

She stands and stares into Lucille's eyes. "Did you know? I love you, Grandma Lucille."

Lucille nods, her throat aching. This always happens. Only a few minutes into the visit and Lucille wants the child to stay forever. She touches Nola's cheek, soft as a pile of sifted flour. "I love you, too."

# Cookie Class

L
UCILLE'S KITCHEN IS LOUD WITH THE SOUNDS of excited children. Seven six-years-olds have gathered for the potato-chip cookie class, and Lucille is letting them release a little nervous energy and excitement before the class begins. Nola is making a neat arrangement of the ingredients that they'll need. At her suggestion, Lucille tied a polka-dot ribbon around the base of the mixer, and affixed a balloon on the door handle to the half-bath. The demo cookies that Nola and Lucille and Maddy made last night (and then ate half of) have already been served to the children from a yellow dump truck; boys and girls alike seem to enjoy having a cookie dumped onto their little paper plates. Today's plates are zoo animals: tigers, lions, elephants, and monkeys. There was a bit of a dustup between two children wanting the last monkey plate, but Nola offered an ingenious

solution: she told the squabbling children that all the plates were monkeys, some were just still wearing their Halloween costumes.

When everything is ready to go, Lucille claps her hands and a silence descends. "Good afternoon!" she says, and waits for the children to sing out, "Good afternoon, Miss Howard," but children are not like that anymore. With rare exception, they say nothing after she greets them. Not their fault, of course, if they haven't been taught basic manners.

"As you know, today I will be showing you how to make potato-chip cookies. How many of you liked the sample you had?"

All hands up. No surprise there. One hand stays up, though. A big blond boy, seated at the back of the class. His name is Parker Daley, and he came to another class last week. His mother was a full forty minutes late picking him up, and her idea of an apology was to say, "Whoops! Guess time got away from me!" Parker's not great about doing the work, he's one of those who starts something and doesn't want to finish, but he's a champion eater.

"Parker?" Lucille says. "Did you have a question?"

"Why can't we make thumbprint cookies?"

"Well, we just did that last week, didn't we?"

"Yeah, but they're better than these cookies today."

"No they're not!" Nola says loudly. "These ones are way better."

"Okay, let's just say that they're both good, shall we?" Lucille says. "Not everybody likes everything the same. Now let's get going. Who can tell me the first thing to do when you're going to bake something?"

"Go poop," Parker says quietly, and the children giggle.

Lucille ignores him. "It's 'wash your hands,' because you don't want anyone getting sick from germs, right? So, let's one at a time come up to the sink, and we're going to make sure our hands are nice and clean."

After the children have returned to their places, Lucille says, "Okay, class, the next thing is to assemble your ingredients."

"Your **pee** and **poop**," Parker says.

Lucille sighs. "Parker?"

He smirks at her.

"Would you come up here, please?"

His smirk disappears. After a second, he gets out of his chair and comes to stand beside her.

"I can see you have the makings of a real leader," Lucille says.

The boy stares up at her.

"So I'm going to ask if you'd be willing to help me."

"I'm your helper!" Nola says.

"Yes, and now Parker is going to help us as well. And, say, Parker, can you whistle?"

"Yes."

"Well, that's good, because we're going to need someone to whistle."

"What for?" Parker asks.

"That's for me to know and you to find out," Lucille says.

Parker studies her, and Lucille knows very well he's deciding whether to abandon his plan for mischief and instead cooperate with her. "A loud whistle?" he asks.

Lucille hands the sticks of butter to Nola to unwrap. "The loudest! I need a whistle so loud it will make everyone's hair stand on end. Can you do it?"

The boy grins. "Sure. When?"

"I'll let you know. I'll give you a special signal. Now, who wants to help mix the butter?"

All hands up.

IT IS JUST AFTER the class has ended that Lucille slips on a butter wrapper that someone left on the floor. She catches herself on the way down, but she falls.

"Grandma!" Nola says.

"I'm all right," Lucille tells her, though she's not sure she is.

Nola squats down beside her. "Should we call the ambulance?"

"I'm all right," Lucille says again, and, to prove it, hoists herself up. "See? I'm okay. Nothing broken."

Nothing may be broken, but something sure hurts in her back. When she hears the front door open and Maddy calling hello, she is so grateful. Talk about good timing. "In here!" she says.

Maddy's smile fades when she sees Lucille. "What happened?"

"She fell **down**!" Nola says.

"I just slipped a little," Lucille says.

"Are you okay?" Maddy asks.

"I'm fine!"

"Can you walk?"

Lucille doesn't move.

"I'm taking you to the hospital," Maddy says.

"I'm fine!"

"Can you walk?"

Lucille rolls her eyes. "For heaven's sake!" **Who's on first?** She lets go of the chair she used to hoist herself up and tries to take a step independently, then cries out.

"Okay," Maddy says. "We'll use the chair to get you out to the car. Use it like a walker, can you? Just slide it and I'll walk behind you."

Lucille makes it to the car, but now her back is screaming. "Nuts," she says quietly. And that is all.

When they arrive at the hospital, the ER is empty, so Lucille is put into a treatment room right away. An hour later, after X-rays and an exam, she is released with prescriptions for muscle relaxers and pain pills, which she will not take. No. She's not going to get addicted. A heating pad and Tylenol will do, and that's what she told them, but they insisted she take the prescriptions. They thought she was in a lot of pain. She pointed to the face on the pain chart that showed the mouth as a straight line, number four, not nearly number ten, but they thought she was hurting more than that because she kept crying. What they didn't know is that she wasn't crying from physical pain. It was for another reason.

Later that night, after Nola has been put to bed and Maddy and Lucille are sitting at the kitchen table in their nightwear—Lucille in her flannel gown featuring floating roses and Maddy in black sweatpants and T-shirt—Lucille says, "You know why I was crying so much in the treatment room?" She adjusts the pillow and heating pad behind her. See? Already better.

"You were scared?" Maddy asks.

"No. I wasn't scared. I was crying because that was the room where Frank died. I was standing right outside the room that night. They wouldn't let me in to be with him."

Maddy's hand flies to her mouth. "Oh, Lucille. I'm so sorry!"

"Yes, that room is where all hope came to an end."

Maddy says nothing and Lucille says, "I guess that was a bit dramatic."

"It's how you feel. Or felt."

"Well, that's right. It is how I felt. And to tell you the truth, Maddy, it's still how I feel. Oh, I'm going on with my life, anyone can see that, but it feels like the center of me has just about withered up. I don't know what I'd do if I didn't have you and Nola."

"You know you have us forever, right? No matter where we are?"

"Yes. I do know that. And I'm very grateful."

Maddy grows quiet and looks around the kitchen. "Do you miss him?"

"Who? Arthur?"

"Yes."

"I do. I think of him sometimes. How about you?"

"I think of him every day," Maddy says. She stares out the window. "I'm not sure if you know this, Lucille, but he saved my life. I was very close to . . . I didn't really want to live for a while. But he was such a radiant soul, and something about him convinced me that life is worth living. That it may not be fair, but it is beautiful. I loved Arthur very much."

"I loved him, too," Lucille says. "Not like I loved Frank, of course, but I loved Arthur. There he would be, quiet at the table, with those long legs crossed, content first thing in the morning and content last thing at night. Why, it was like a **scent** he gave off."

"I know," Maddy says, smiling. "Remember how he used to fall asleep in front of the TV when we were watching old movies and then deny that he'd been sleeping? 'I wasn't sleeping, I was dozing,' he'd say. **Dozing** with his mouth hanging open and head cocked all funny!"

"And snoring," Lucille says.

Maddy doesn't mention the fact that Lucille snores louder than two Arthurs put together.

"Lucille? You know how you say Frank was the love of your life?"

"Yes. He was."

"I never told you, but I used to think that was kind of silly."

Lucille raises her eyebrows, nods. She points to Maddy's engagement ring. "Different story now, huh?"

"Different story."

Maddy stands and pushes her chair under the table. "Let's get you into bed. And we'll see how you are tomorrow. I'm not going home if you're not better."

"I'm better already," Lucille says. She's not that much better, but she won't have Maddy missing school. Maybe she'll ask to dream of Frank tonight.

After she has turned her bedside lamp out, Lucille looks over at her glow-in-the-dark alarm clock. Lately, she draws comfort from watching the second hand go smoothly around and around. Isn't it funny that she, so enamored of the past, is now consoled by seeing time move relentlessly forward? It's as though she's dying for something to finally come.

A few hours later, Lucille becomes aware of a figure next to her bed. She sits up rapidly, and the movement hurts her back. "Ouch!" she says, and then, "Frank?"

"No, ma'am, I'm not Frank."

It's that damned angel again.

"Lucille Rachel Howard—"

"Save yourself a speech," Lucille says. "I'm not ready, I told you before." Her anger rouses, she feels her heart begin to pound forcefully in her chest.

"Go away!" she says, and he does.

"For cripe's sake," Lucille says, and lies back down. "I want to dream of **Frank**!"

She closes her eyes, falls asleep again, and guess what. He is wearing a white shirt and khaki pants. His silver hair is shining. He's chewing gum and leaning against his red Cadillac with his arms crossed, waiting. "Yoo-hoo!" she calls, but her voice is very soft and muffled; her jaw won't unclench. She tries to run to him, but her legs won't move. "Frank!" she calls again, and then her eyes open and it is morning and she is looking at the second hand of her clock going around and around. This is now, and she is still here.

# And That's for **You!**

---

TINY OPENS THE BACK DOOR OF HIS TRUCK for his diminutive customer, one Ollie Futters, who is in her nineties if she's a day, but she makes a point of not revealing her age. "If I told you how old I was, you'd find me less attractive," she once told Tiny, chuckling.

He waits patiently as Ollie gets ready to climb out of the truck. First her cane comes out; then, after a great deal of time, she's ready for an arm to assist her. Tiny carries her groceries up to her front door. She buys the same thing every week: mostly frozen dinners, but also Special K, a jug of milk, a carton of half-and-half, a bunch of bananas, a bag of prunes, two rolls of Charmin. She also always has a bag from Sugarbutter with one blueberry muffin and one cheese Danish and one maple cruller in it. That's because whenever Tiny gets a call from Ollie saying she needs to go to the grocery store, he heads over to the bakery before he picks her up; he knows what kind of pastry she really likes. Each time, she offers to pay him; each time, he refuses. And then Ollie will say, as she always does, "Well, I guess I **am** your best customer, aren't I?"

She isn't, not by a long shot. Each week, after Tiny has helped her out of the truck, carried her groceries in and put them away, she'll pay the minuscule fare, then press a quarter firmly into his hand and say, "And that's for **you,** cabbie!" That's exactly what she does now, her hand trembling.

"Thanks, Ollie," Tiny says, pocketing the coin.

"Think nothing of it," she says. And then, "Would you like to stay for dinner?"

It's not unusual for her to ask. Tiny has had dinner with her a few times, usually a Swanson fried chicken dinner, which Tiny finds delicious if insubstantial. They always watch sports while the food cooks, and Ollie is happiest when wrestling is on. But this is Wednesday, and Tiny and Dan are meeting at the Alarm Bell, and so he declines Ollie's offer.

"I'm getting lucky tonight," Dan had told him. "I can feel it. She'll be a redhead, too. She'll be sitting at the bar, drinking a cosmo, and when we come in, she'll turn around and see me and that will be that. Boom."

"Congratulations," Tiny said, and Dan said, "Hey. Don't jinx it."

It's nearly eight o'clock before Dan is ready to throw in the towel at the Alarm Bell. "Slim pickings tonight," he says. "And I was so sure."

They have just laid down their money to pay the check when a tall redhead walks in, surveys the room, and takes the empty seat next to Tiny. She orders a cosmo. Tiny looks wide-eyed over at Dan, then hops off the stool and heads for the bathroom. He'll give them a chance to talk; there's no one else sitting at the bar, the place is dead tonight. But when he comes out, Dan is waiting at the door for him. Tiny looks over at the woman, then at Dan, questioningly. Dan scowls, shakes his head, and they walk outside.

"What happened?" Tiny asks, once they're in the truck.

"Nothing happened." A sulky moment, and then Dan says, "Why do they always sit by you?"

Tiny shrugs. "I don't know."

"They always sit by you. They always talk to you. Never me."

"Sometimes you."

"Yeah. That redhead, she talked to me."

"Why didn't you stay, then?"

"'Cause here's how she talked to me. She said, 'What's your friend's name? He's cute.'" Dan looks over at him. "You ain't any cuter than I am."

"Neither one of us is any prize," Tiny says.

"You always do something to take their attention off me," Dan says.

"I don't do anything!"

"I think you're jealous of me and so you try to sabotage me with the ladies."

"I'm not jealous of you, Dan. And I'm not interested in any of your ladies."

"Yeah, you are."

Tiny sighs.

They sit in silence for a while. Then Tiny says, "Want to try another place?"

"Let's just call it a night."

Tiny starts his truck. "Good idea."

# A Little Dinner Party

IRIS KNOCKS ON TINY'S DOOR, HOPING FOR three things. One is that he's home. Another is that he doesn't mind unscheduled visits. The third is that he's glad the visitor is Iris.

He flings open the door. Then his face lights up and he says, "Iris!" A sweep.

"C'mon in," he says. "Excuse the smell. I'm cooking onions."

"Smells good. What are you making?"

"Onions."

"For . . ."

"For eating!" He goes over to the stove to push around the onions with a fork. He has a dishtowel stuck into his britches, another flung over his shoulder. Onion peels are all over the counter. He has the radio on, tuned to a country station, some she-done-me-wrong song playing that he sings along with.

Tiny looks over his shoulder. "You like country music?"

Iris nods. "I do. I like every kind of music."

"I used to love this one song that goes, '**You just sorta stomped on my aorta.**' You ever hear that one?"

She smiles. "Nope."

"Take your coat off! Stay for supper! I'm making hamburgers. Do you like hamburgers? With onions?"

"Absolutely." Iris takes off her coat and lays it neatly over the back of a tan Naugahyde sofa, though calling it a sofa is like calling a skyscraper a yurt. It's one of the ugliest pieces of furniture Iris has ever seen and also the type that she has lusted after for years. It has recliners built in at either end and it has a little tabletop built into the middle section to put food and drinks on, and you can lift the tabletop up to reveal a storage place. She knows all this because she and Ed once looked at one of these sofas. It was at a gigantic furniture warehouse, one of those places where you would be hard-pressed to find a piece of tasteful furniture, but you couldn't beat the prices— and they gave away free popcorn in little striped boxes with scalloped edges. She and Ed went there for the popcorn, truth be told—they'd been to a clothing store nearby. So they were strolling around, eating popcorn, and they came upon that sofa and mirthfully locked eyes. They sat at either end, and they couldn't stop grinning. It was so comfortable! It was so much fun! It was like going on a ride that didn't move! And, bonus: who cared if nacho grease or chocolate or hair balls from the cat got on it? Then a saleswoman came over, blouse halfway untucked from a too-tight skirt, a pencil stuck behind her ear, asking if they were interested in adding this to their collection.

They leaped up together, shame-faced. Iris said, "Oh, no thank you, we're just looking," at the same time that Ed said, "How much would you charge to deliver this thing?" In the end, they didn't buy it; neither of them **really** wanted it, but Ed had for a moment almost succumbed to the absolute inge- niousness of the thing. Now, sinking down onto the end of Tiny's sofa, pulling the lever to make the recliner pop out, and settling her head against the rise that served as a pillow, she thinks they should have.

"Pretty comfortable, huh?" Tiny says, coming out of the kitchen.

"Yes!"

"Ugly as hell, though."

"Well . . ."

"It is! But man, you can cozy down in that thing. You get yourself some snacks and sit down and you don't ever have to get up."

"I almost bought one once, years ago."

"Is that right?"

Back to Ed. She doesn't want to go back to Ed. So she says, "Hey, remember those interviews I told you I was going for? I got one of the jobs."

"Hold on a minute, let me stir the onions."

When he returns to the living room, he says, "Which one?"

"It's to be an assistant for a woman who teaches baking classes."

"Who, Lucille Howard?"

"Yes! Do you know her?"

"Sure, I know almost everybody in this town. She's a good baker, I've had her stuff. One night, I gave her a ride home from the supermarket, she doesn't like to drive at night. I carried her bags in for her and she gave me some muffins, lemon-blueberry ones, and man, they were good. So you're going to help her teach?"

"Well, I got the impression that she doesn't need any help teaching. I got that impression because she told me not to get **any** ideas about interacting directly with the students."

Tiny shakes his head. "Yeah, old Lucille. But you know, she's—"

"Oh, I like her!" Iris says. "I'm going to do some things on the computer for her. She doesn't have a website. Or a computer, for that matter."

"I can't believe Lucille Howard is getting a website!"

"Neither can she. Just as I was about to go out the door, she said, 'I wonder if you could do that thing where you put pictures on it.' It was as though she were saying, 'I wonder if you could do that thing where you split the atom.' I told her it was no problem, we could even put videos of her teaching on there, and she thought that was just wonderful. Though, 'No shots of me from behind!' she said."

"When do you start?"

"Tomorrow."

Iris sniffs at the air. "I think your onions are burning.

"Yeah, we'll let 'em burn a little more and then we'll pile 'em up on the burgers. I'll start the burgers now. I make Juicy Lucys, stuffed with cheese and jalapeños—you like jalapeños?"

"I do."

"I'm sorry to say I don't have any chips."

"I've got chips," Iris says, putting her recliner in the upright position. "I'll go and get them."

"They ain't those **light** ones, are they?"

"Forty-percent reduced fat?"

"Uh . . ."

"Okay, tell you what. I'll bring some ice cream over instead, for dessert. Full-fat."

"Now you're talking. And just so you know, this is my last big meal for a while. Tomorrow: Lean Cuisine, all the way. Thirty days and then I'm going to ask Monica out. I got it all figured out. I'll take her to a play with live actors. That'll surprise her! She'll never see that one coming! And then we'll go out for a late-night dinner. Real romantic."

"Oh, that's great. Which play?"

"I don't know. One a woman would like. Maybe you can help me pick one out."

"I'd be glad to."

"Maybe you could weigh in on the restaurant, too."

"Okay."

"And . . . I don't think my clothes will fit too well if my plan works, so . . ."

"We'll go to a department store. I need some clothes, too."

"Iris?"

"Yes?"

"I'm real happy you moved in."

"I am, too."

"Go and get the ice cream."

"Okay."

She nearly skips going down the hall, and what she is remembering is a friend of hers who suffered from depression. That friend told Iris that there were times when she was feeling desperate and she'd go out to the mall and buy a lipstick and feel better. And she would wonder how serious her depression could be if a lipstick could lift her spirits in that way. Iris asked what kind of lipstick her friend bought and her friend said Chanel. And Iris said, "Well, no wonder." Tiny is offering only a hamburger, but it is Chanel. And so is he.

She pulls a quart of chocolate-cherry-walnut ice cream from the freezer. It's from Willigan's, the town's little ice cream parlor, and it's the best ice cream she's ever tasted. She spies a bag of curly fries, and grabs them, too. Also she'll bring a couple of bananas and some chocolate syrup and some nuts and a can of whipped cream. **See that?** she thinks. **You take one step of pure and good intention and the universe accommodates.**

She can hear Ed now, saying something like he always used to say when she mentioned "the universe" in that way. He would say something that was the verbal equivalent of holding your nose.

So, right, she doesn't miss everything.

When they are eating dinner, Iris says, "If you could do what seems like an impossible thing, what would it be?"

"Lose weight," Tiny says. "Lose about fifty, sixty pounds and then ask Monica Mayhew to marry me."

Iris's eyes widen. "Really?"

"Might be a tad soon."

"Especially since you've never even asked her out."

Tiny's brow wrinkles. "Right. Zero times. Too scared she'll say no. I'm pretty sure she'll say no. And then that would be the end of . . . Well, it would be the end of everything. I wouldn't even be able to go to the Henhouse anymore."

"Tiny! Don't you know she has a big crush on you? It's written all over her! And she asked **you** out! Remember? She asked if you'd like to go to a movie sometime. And you told **her** no!"

"Yeah, I know. I panicked. I thought I should do the hard-to-get thing, like my friend Dan suggested. It was stupid. And then later that day I thought, I know, I'll call her back and say . . . Well, that's the problem. I didn't know what to say. Seems like when things are too important, you don't know what to say."

"Tiny, I think I can help you with Monica, if you'd like."

"You'd make better suggestions than Dan, being a girl and all."

A **girl.** What a lovely notion.

"Maybe it would be easier to double-date, the first time. Maybe with Dan?"

"Dan and I are on the outs."

"Oh? Why is that?"

"He told me I get in the way of him and women. So, you know . . . He's kind of disappeared from my life for a while."

"Well, I'm here," Iris says. "And I think you'd look great in a blue shirt that matches your eyes."

Tiny looks down at his plate. "Yeah?"

# Abby

———

O N THE MORNING OF NOVEMBER 4, ABBY wakes up and lies still for a moment. It has become her habit to try to think of something she's grateful for before getting up to face another day of chemo. It's a good practice; it helps.

Today, she thinks of how glad she is for this house, and for Mason, this funny little town. She's particularly grateful for the friendliness of the people who live here, the manageability of the place, the slower pace. She fits right in with a slower pace these days. No more five-mile jogs with Jason every morning. "In a year, we'll get it up to seven miles," Jason said last night, as they lay in bed holding hands. And although a dark voice in Abby's brain said, **I'll be dead in a year,** she told Jason, "Ten."

She takes in a deep breath and sits up. It is her habit to make the bed as soon as she's out of it, or even before, as she does now, turning to fluff the pillows before standing. But she sees a dark clump on her pillow and gasps. At first she thinks it's some kind of animal. But then she sees what it is, and puts her hand to her head, and more hair comes off. A pale-blue pamphlet, offering information about what to expect with chemotherapy and affecting a position somewhere between cheer and solemnity: **You may lose the hair on your head, as well as your eyelashes, eyebrows, and pubic hair.**

For a moment, she sits still as a statue at the edge of the bed. Then tears spring to her eyes and she crosses her arms tightly and begins to rock back and forth. She puts the fallen-out hair in her lap and strokes it, it is thick, shiny dark-auburn hair, and now it looks like a bird's wing. She looks out the window as the light suddenly pushes through, and she finds that so beautiful, and part of the beauty is that it has nothing to do with her. The sun has been rising and setting for so long and will continue to rise and set long after she is gone, whatever the cause of her death. Long after everyone on the earth today is gone, here will come the sun, there will run the rivers, and the songs of birds will fill the air. She will not think of the entropy that everyone predicts, not now, because these days nature is her religion. And **Black Elk Speaks** is her Bible, she has always loved that book, and its theme of a spiritual journey has special meaning to her now. She likes the way the book teaches that you are only one part of a greater whole. That idea gives her strength, she told Jason, and he said, Good, I'm glad it does. And then he pinched the bridge of his nose, which is something he does when he feels he is near tears.

Downstairs, she can hear Jason making breakfast for Lincoln, and she hears him call. "Linky! Come down right now, or you'll be late for school!"

"Coming!" Lincoln says, and then there is noise of him going downstairs, his backpack bumping along behind him. He is too old to keep a stuffed animal in his backpack, but he does anyway, a little calico cat with green eyes, curled up in a circle. None of the other kids know, and Abby is glad, because even though Lincoln has said he wouldn't care if they did know (this after Abby proposed making the cat a secret hiding place), she knows he'd be humiliated. Even here, in a town far more innocent and generous-hearted—and, okay, behind the times—than the one they left, kids would make fun of him.

She won't go downstairs until after Lincoln leaves. Sometimes she makes it down in time to see him off, sometimes she doesn't; he's grown used to this, without knowing what the reason for it is. It breaks her heart how accepting children can be—must be.

She'll have to tell him today. She'll do it after school. She was hoping the ice cap she wore during treatments would let her keep her hair; she was told that half of the time, it works, but it did not work for her. **Oh, well,** she thinks, **it's past time to tell him, anyway.** Once, he came upon her throwing up and said, "Do you have the flu?" and she'd nodded, then said, "Just a little twenty-four-hour one, I'm sure. I'll be okay."

She wipes her eyes and stands to finish making the bed, pulling the sheets tightly, forming the hospital corners her mother taught her. She runs her hand over the compass quilt she's using as a bedspread, it's such a beautiful piece of work and she loves sleeping under it because sometimes she wakes up a little afraid in the night and it comforts her to touch something her mother touched. When it's big fear, she turns to Jason and holds him close and he awakens and does not say a word and so speaks volumes.

She hears the front door slam, Lincoln going out to catch the bus. She showers, brushes her teeth, dresses, and puts on a little lip gloss to go downstairs. Normal is what she's after.

"Hey, sweetheart," Jason says, when she comes into the kitchen. He's wiping off the table, sweeping crumbs into his hand. He looks up at her and smiles. And then he stops smiling.

"Yeah," she says. "It's happening." In the shower, a great deal more hair had fallen out. She'd collected it from where it had gathered near the drain, tossed it in the garbage, then pulled it out, wrapped it in a washcloth, and put it in her nightstand drawer. She doesn't know what to do with it.

Jason stands there. Swallows. She thinks of something a friend of hers once told her, that when you recite Kaddish as a mourner, you stand, while everyone else in the congregation remains seated.

"It's okay," she says.

"It's only hair, right?"

"Right."

"It will come back," he says.

"Three to six months after the treatment ends."

"Right. So, that's not so bad!" He's trying hard, but his voice is tight.

He comes over to embrace her, and then he is weeping and so is she, but all she says is, "Uh-oh. You dropped the crumbs on the floor."

"MOM!" LINCOLN YELLS THAT afternoon, after he comes into the house.

"In here," Abby says. She's sitting at the kitchen table with Jason. She's wearing the prettiest scarf on her head, something she'd not worn until now, but it's lovely, all greens and blues and golds.

Lincoln comes into the kitchen. "Hi."

"Hi, sweetheart."

"Can I go to Mike Pizer's house?"

"Sure, but can we talk to you for just a minute?"

He looks from one to the other. "What'd I do?"

"Nothing," Abby says. "We just have some news we want to share. Sit down. You want something to eat? An apple? Some cheese?"

"No thanks. And I know what your news is."

Abby's stomach clenches and she steals a quick look at Jason, who has taken her hand beneath the table.

"Do you?"

"Yeah. I'm going to have a baby brother. Or sister."

"Ah," Abby says. "That's a good guess. But it's not that."

"What is it, then?"

"Well, I need to tell you that I have cancer, Lincoln."

He stares at her. Then he says loudly, "What do you mean? Are you sick? What do you **mean**, Mom? What is cancer, anyway? Like what **is** it?"

"That's a very good question. Because cancer is just one word that can mean many things. Sometimes cancer is such a little thing, and other times it's a bit more serious. I have cancer that is a bit more serious, but I am getting treatments to get better."

"Is that why you've been so tired? And throwing up?"

She nods. "Um-hm. It's not fun, but it's how we know the medicine is working."

Lincoln stares down at the table. "Fuck," he says softly.

"**Linky** . . ." Jason says, and Lincoln looks directly at him and Jason says no more.

"Are you going to die?" Lincoln asks, and this is a question Abby was anticipating. Even so, it takes everything in her to tell him the truth and say, "I'm going to try really hard not to. I think I will be fine. And so does Dad. And you should think that, too, okay?"

He looks at her face as though it is a map he's studying in order to locate a certain city. He looks at her eyes, her mouth, her nose, he looks up at the scarf on her head with new understanding.

"Are you bald now?"

"Not yet. But my hair has begun to fall out. Do you want to see?"

"No."

Silence, and then Lincoln says, "You should just do a buzz cut, if it's going to fall out."

"Maybe," she says. "It might look kind of cool." And then, "Linky, I might have to do some other treatments over in Columbia, near to where we go to the bookstore. If I do that, and Dad comes with me, which I would want him to, it would mean we wouldn't be here when you got back from school. So we'll need to find—"

"I don't need a babysitter."

"Yes you do, son," Jason says.

"I'm fine by myself!"

"You are, but we would want someone here just in case. Or we would want you to go someplace where there was an adult."

"What about Miss Howard next door? She's always home. She could be there if I needed anything."

A little jump of happiness in Abby, and she says, "Would that feel okay for you? If you stayed with her?"

"Yeah, I could just go over there if I needed her."

"Well, you'd need to stay there," Abby says. "Actually."

"Tell you what," Jason says. "How about I take your mom out for a while tonight and you stay with

Miss Howard for just an hour or so, and you can see how it feels. We asked her if she'd do that and she said sure. She said she was making spaghetti and meatballs for dinner and you could join her."

"We don't eat meat."

"Right, but you could have some sauce."

"That meat was cooked in?"

"Yeah, if you're okay with it. Otherwise you could have the spaghetti with just cheese."

"I eat meat, you know. At school, when they have fried chicken, kids share it with me. It's **good**!"

"Well," Abby says, "it—"

Jason squeezes her hand. **Don't.**

"It's fine for now," Abby says.

"Really?"

"Yes."

"So I can have meatballs?"

"Eat whatever you like," Jason says.

Abby can't help it. She says, "But, you know, try to make good choices."

"Can I go to Mike's house now?"

"Yes, but be back at five. Miss Howard eats early."

# A New Friend for Lucille

ONE THING LUCILLE JUST KNOWS LINCOLN will love is garlic bread, because she loved garlic bread as a kid. They'll have spaghetti and meatballs and garlic bread and a little salad and then she'll offer dessert, even though they don't eat dessert over there. But she'll offer it, it's a blueberry-peach crisp with an oatmeal-based topping, so it's healthy. Healthy enough. She won't push it, she'll just say, "I'm going to have some delicious blueberry-peach crisp, would you like some, too?" Then, if he says yes, she'll plop a little ice cream on there and if he says anything about that, she'll say, "Well, it comes with that." Then he'll taste it and that will do it.

She has cleared this with the parents. With the father, anyway. Jeremy. Is it Jeremy? No. **Jason.** She told him what was on the menu and asked if that would be all right to give Lincoln and he said it would be fine. He was a little distracted, but he heard her.

Poor man. He could not care less about what his son has for dinner. He's worried about his wife. She's got some kind of medical problem, and he asked Lucille if she would be at all amenable to letting Lincoln come over after school sometimes. Wouldn't be for more than a couple of hours at a time.

Lucille was not wildly excited about the idea, at first. She doesn't even know the kid, for one thing, but she likes kids generally, or she never could have taught fourth grade for all those years, even though that wretched Krissy Labrue nearly did her in, her third year of teaching. You never want to think of one of your students as a little shit, but that's just what that child was. Lucille tried to tender her resignation three times that academic year, and each time was persuaded not to, because everyone else thought the girl was a royal pain, too. But Lucille is sure she'll like Lincoln well enough. And anyway, neighbors do for each other, Arthur taught her that.

She looks at her watch, then goes into her bathroom to freshen up. You'd think she was getting ready for a date.

A date. The idea makes her sit down on the toilet seat and sigh. **Frank.**

She gets up and puts on lipstick and runs a brush through her hair, not that the boy will care what her hair looks like. Kids don't really see old people. A lot of people don't.

The doorbell rings and she goes downstairs. Jason

is standing at the door with his hand on Lincoln's shoulder. The boy looks up at her shyly and Lucille's heart instantly goes to him.

"Come on in," she says. "Welcome! Are you ready for some dinner?"

"I guess so," he says. "Thank you."

"And then I have plans for after-dinner entertainment."

"What?"

"It's a surprise. I like surprises, don't you?"

"I don't know. I guess it depends on what the surprise is."

"You'll like it," she says, putting her hand gently on his shoulder to guide him in. "You skedaddle," she tells Jason.

"We'll see you in an hour, son," Jason says, and Lucille says, "Oh, we're going to need at least two."

Jason looks down at Lincoln and the boy grins. "I'm fine, Dad."

"IS THERE SUGAR IN HERE?" Lincoln asks, about the crisp, after taking a bite.

"Well, of course. What would crisp be without sugar? Horse feed."

"My family doesn't eat sugar."

"Yes, I know. I did ask your dad if you could try this, though. And he didn't seem to mind."

"Yeah. I can eat whatever I want now, because my mom has cancer."

Lucille makes herself not react much. "I'm very sorry to hear that, Lincoln."

"Yeah. She's going to get better, I think."

"Yes. She's young, and she's healthy. I mean, otherwise."

"She might die, though."

What to say. Absurdly, the cuckoo clock in her kitchen strikes.

"What's **that**?" Lincoln asks.

"It's a cuckoo clock," Lucille says. "Haven't you ever seen a cuckoo clock?"

"No."

"Well, every hour the little bird comes out of his house and cuckoos once for every hour that it is."

"Wow. Twelve o'clock must be awesome!"

"I can make it do that."

"Would you?"

"'Course I would. Let me get out my little ladder. Now, I want you to spot me, and I'll climb up and make it cuckoo twelve times, just for you." Thank goodness her back pain is gone.

She hauls out her stepladder from the pantry and climbs up a step, then two, with Lincoln close behind her and with one of her hands on top of his head to steady her. She moves the hands of the clock to make the bird cuckoo and cuckoo and cuckoo and they both laugh themselves silly. One good thing about someone really liking something you have is that you appreciate it yourself all over again. It is funny, isn't it, the little door snapping open, the bird popping out and then quickly back in, the door slamming behind him.

After she's made it cuckoo twelve o'clock three times, she says, "All right, that's enough, I'm getting a little dizzy. Help me down and then we're going to do our entertainment."

"I think I know what it is."

"No you don't."

"Is it a movie?"

That wouldn't have been a bad idea, Lucille thinks. She could have taken a load off, maybe dozed a bit, and been done with her duties until the parents came back. But she has another idea. It came to her as she was napping that afternoon and so she knows it will work out fine: things that suggest themselves in sleep almost always work out.

"No," she tells Lincoln. "It's not a movie. Come, and I'll show you."

He looks at the dishes on the table. "Shouldn't we clean up first?"

"You want to help me clean up?"

"Sure."

"Well, aren't you just Sir Lancelot!"

"Who's that?"

"Oh, he was a gallant knight in King Arthur's court. You know what a knight is, don't you?"

"Yeah. They were in the Middle Ages. They wore suits of armor."

"That's right. Very good."

She stations herself at the sink. "Bring me over the dishes, and I'll wash them."

"You don't have a dishwasher?"

She looks over her shoulder. "It's a wonder I survive, right?"

He shrugs.

She takes the plate he hands her and begins soaping it. "I don't mind washing dishes. I think about things when I do. Don't you like to do that sometimes, just be doing something kind of mindless and think about things, let your imagination wander?"

"I don't know. I guess. What was that knight's name, again?"

"Lancelot."

"I like that name."

"It's a little bit like your name."

She rinses a fork and puts it in the drainer. "Do you like your name?"

"Yeah, 'cept when my parents call me Linky, which I'm too old for now."

"Tell them to call you Lincoln, then."

He's silent.

"You can tell them to call you Lincoln."

"I would want them to call me Link."

"Oh! Link. Yes, that's quite nice. Very elegant. So tell them to call you Link. And get that dishtowel that's hanging over there. You might as well dry."

"What do you mean?"

"Dry the dishes! With the dishtowel!"

He stands there.

"Pretend the dishes have just come out of the bathtub and now you are going to dry them."

"Oh. Okay." He gets the dishtowel and wraps it around a wet plate and starts pressing here and there.

"Lord have mercy," Lucille says, and snatches the plate away. "Like this!" she says, and shows him how to dry a dish. She read in the paper the other day that a mom had to tell her college-age son how to mail a letter. True story.

"So, Link," she says.

He smiles.

"You like how it sounds?"

"Yeah."

"All right, so from now on, I'll call you Link and you tell your parents to do it, too."

"Maybe later. They're kind of upset right now."

She rinses a glass, puts it in the drainer, and keeps her voice purposefully casual to say, "I really think your mom will be just fine."

"But you don't know."

"No, I don't."

"Nobody knows."

They work in silence but for the squeaking of the dishrag, and then Lincoln says, "Do you believe in heaven?"

"Of course I do."

"For real?"

"Yes! Don't you?"

"I think it's an artificial construct. That's what my dad says."

"Is that so. I'll bet you don't even know what 'artificial construct' means."

"It means it's a fake idea. People make up heaven so they won't be scared to die."

"That's not true!"

"How do you know?"

"How do you know **not**?"

He looks up at her, confused.

"Let me ask you something," Lucille says. "Will the sun come up tomorrow?"

"Yeah . . ."

"How do you know?"

He laughs. "Because it just does. Every day, the sun comes up."

"But how do you know it will come up tomorrow? Put that silverware away in the top drawer over there, will you?"

He gathers the silverware that he has dried and laid on the table, and puts it in the drawer, carefully. She might hire him to help with her classes. He's smart, he's considerate, he's so cute with his red hair and freckles and big brown eyes. She's hired that Iris woman now to set up all kinds of Internet nonsense, but this kid could probably have done it. He's one of those really smart ones, she knows one when she sees one.

"How do you **know** the sun will come up?" she asks him again.

"Because the earth spins—"

"You know the sun will come up because you have faith that it will. That's how you know. And that's how I know about heaven, because of my faith. And that's all I'm going to say about it, this is not the Pentecostal Jamboree.

"Tell you what, let's let the pans soak and go into the living room and have some fun. Know what we're going to do? We're going to build a city from playing cards."

"No way," he says. And Lucille, feeling as cool as if she's wearing a motorcycle jacket, says, "Way."

In the living room, Lucille takes out two decks of cards and gives him one. She shows him how to balance one card against another to make walls, how, if you're careful, you can put a roof on and then build up. "Now, you go on the floor over there, and I'll do my city on the coffee table."

Lincoln sits down, leans a card against a chair to get started, and then they are both lost in their respective enterprises. When Lucille looks up, she sees that Lincoln has constructed a pretty impressive tower. She is just about to compliment him on it when it collapses. He turns around to look at her, exasperated, and she shrugs.

"I'm going to do it again, another way."

Yup, smart kid.

Lincoln has nearly completed another structure when the doorbell rings. "Oh, no," he says. "I'm not done!"

"Next time," Lucille says, and walks with Lincoln to the door to deliver him to his father. "Bring him back anytime," she says, and watches them walk over to their house. She sees Abby at the window, a scarf on her head. Lord. She'll make them red lentil soup with apricot, and a hearty root-vegetable stew and whole-wheat dinner rolls. She'll do whatever she can, especially when it comes to little Lancelot.

Really, she can't wait for next time. They'll have macaroni and cheese and green beans and raspberry custard pie and watch an old Western, maybe with Gene Autry, whom she **still** has a crush on. She has never known a problem that spending time with cowboys didn't help, if only a little. She's going to get some bubble gum to be their chewin' tobaccy. Also, somewhere in the back of her closet she has a cowboy hat. It belonged to Arthur Moses. He never did get to wear it, so let Link. She'll teach him "Don't Fence Me In." She can't abide the music most kids listen to these days. Rap is crap, if you ask Lucille. She'll teach him to sing, **"Let me be by myself in the evenin' breeze / And listen to the murmur of the cotton- wood trees."**

When she lies down, she immediately drifts off to sleep.

# Set an Attractive Place

Tiny sets his bag of groceries on the
kitchen counter and slowly unpacks it. Sure
are a lot of fruits and vegetables. He got some
chicken breasts and some frozen fish, too. But nothing good. No chips, no dip, no cookies or pies or
coffee cakes or doughnuts. He didn't even buy popcorn for snacking, because it was too confusing
trying to figure out what kind to buy. There's not
one thing here that makes him feel like diving in
and eating. Nothing.

**Set an attractive place,** the website for weight loss
told him. **Even if you're dining alone, make yourself
welcome at your own table. Put a pretty flower next
to your plate, use a lovely cloth napkin and your
best china.**

Tiny doesn't have any china. He buys his dishes
from the Goodwill and doesn't mind at all that

almost nothing matches. He's not about to buy cloth napkins, and although he likes flowers, he's not going to buy a bouquet for himself. What he has are some perfectly good white paper napkins which he now puts on the table next to his plate. He lays down mismatched silverware, and centers a glass directly over the knife, as instructed. Then he stands back, hands on his hips, and looks to see if the place setting looks inviting.

No, it does not.

What's inviting at a place setting is a plate piled high with roast beef and mashed potatoes and gravy, that's what's inviting. A wedge salad sitting next to a thick cut of prime rib and a loaded bako, that's inviting. A big bowl of thick-cut chips alongside a big bowl of onion dip, that's inviting. And a big slab of warm apple pie, drowning in ice cream, with caramel sauce and whipped cream, that's the most inviting of all.

He sighs and goes into the kitchen to see what to make for dinner. Iris told him to buy some Brussels sprouts, cut them in half, and toss them in a little olive oil and roast the hell out of them, they're ever so tasty. He can't imagine that's true. But he'll try it. A spinach salad with strawberries is really good, too, Iris said, but Tiny can't do that. Those two things don't even go together. One needs to be in cream sauce to be any good; the other needs to be stuck between two layers of shortcake and topped with whipped cream. Then talk to him about spinach and strawberries.

He turns on the TV so he can listen to the hockey game and prepares the sprouts, puts them in the oven along with a chicken breast. One chicken breast with no breading. Just by itself, as wan as could be. He never really thought of a chicken breast as a dead animal, he thought of a chicken breast as fried and as a fine accompaniment to waffles drenched in maple syrup, but this chicken breast looks like a dead animal. Poor little clucker.

So. A dead chicken, Brussels sprouts, and one half-cup of rice. That's his dinner. That and about thirty-five glasses of water.

He'll starve. He'll be dead by tomorrow morning.

Iris, who is always going on and off diets, told him he maybe should enter into this dieting business a bit more gradually. But he said no, he meant business, and he wanted results quickly. He's going to quit eating and start exercising.

"Do you really think Monica cares if you lose weight?" Iris asked him.

Tiny figured Iris might be thinking that Monica is no lightweight herself, she could stand to lose a few pounds. But to Tiny, she is perfect. A man dreams of holding a woman who looks like that. He could save a lot of women a lot of grief if he could persuade them of what he thinks is obvious: they diet for one another.

He told Iris, "I don't think Monica cares if I lose weight, but I do. I want to be in shape for her. I want to take care of her. Way I'm going, I'm going to take myself right out in a few years. Heart attack, diabetes. I know all that. I just needed to feel like I had a reason to get in shape. I'm ready to try."

Tiny makes himself rice, then goes to sit on the sofa and watch the game while the chicken and sprouts cook. But then he quickly stands up and marches in place and feels like an idiot. After he's out of breath, he goes to the bathroom and pees **again**—that damn water!

The kitchen timer sounds. Used to be when the timer sounded to let him know his meal was ready, he would feel a kind of happy uptick inside. Not tonight. Tonight, it feels like grim duty calls.

He sits at the table, spreads his napkin evenly onto his lap. Clears his throat. Then he leaps up and turns on the radio to the classical station. Piano. Kind of pretty. He wonders if Monica likes classical music. He pulls himself as close to the table as his gut will allow, sits up super straight, and starts eating. He takes the recommended **small bites!** which means that he cuts the sprouts in quarters. Looks like he's going to have to add a microscope to his table setting.

The Brussels sprouts aren't nearly as bad as he thought they'd be. Which is not to say that they're really good. He gets the Tabasco sauce and sprinkles some on to help them out a little, and that's what it does, it helps them out a **little**. He puts Tabasco on the chicken, on the rice. He eats everything in less than two minutes, then sits staring at his plate. And then, by God, he picks it up and licks it.

Now what.

**Make sure you get out and about! Move! Take a walk, take a class, meet a friend for coffee, go and get a book you're dying to read.**

He can't meet a friend for coffee—he'll want pie. Plus the friend he's most comfortable with is missing in action. He doesn't know of any classes he might take. The library is closed. He guesses he could take another walk, he took one this morning and it wasn't too bad. He didn't get far, three blocks, and that was it.

Tonight, he'll go four. Pretty soon, he'll be able to go somewhere besides the feed store to buy britches. He'll be able to buy a pair of regular-size khakis. Maybe throw in a belt that isn't the length of the Mississippi River. Maybe throw in an engagement ring, too, with a diamond as bright as the sun.

When he comes home, he eats an apple the way the website told him to, all cut up (**feels like more that way!**), and he eats it with a toothpick, not a confetti-topped one, like they said, but still. And they're right. It lasts longer. It feels more like something. But it does not now and never will feel like dessert. How about this for dessert? A dream of Monica in a yellow dress.

# Monica Gets a Man

—

Monica calls the order in: "Grilled coffee roll, drown it in cow paste. And two chicks and hanger steak on the hoof, whole-wheat shingles."

"Got it!" Roberto says, in a cheerful, birdy tone that, frankly, Monica resents. She herself has been depressed for a while now, ever since she and Polly came back from New Orleans. In her heart is a black tick-tocking, a sense that time is passing and she has got to get going on finding someone else. Tiny has been in twice with that woman Iris, and the last three times he came in alone and sat at the counter, where Janelle waited on him.

Monica doesn't tell anyone how she feels. It doesn't show, either. Dimpled smiles for everyone, a cheerful refilling of coffee endless times for endless customers, **Thanks a bunch!** written on every check, a little bouquet of three daisies drawn beside it. She comes to work on time; she stays for as long as she's needed; if someone tells a joke, she says, **Ha-ha-ha.** Tiny says hello to her when he comes in, but that's it. **Well, hello, Monica,** in that way that used to zip up her spine and make her think he cared for her, or was interested in her, but she guesses now that she was wrong. Maybe he and Iris have a thing going on, even though anyone can see that Monica is a much better match for him.

"You might have to start all over again in the boyfriend department," Polly said. "But that could be a good thing."

Maybe Polly was right. The fortune-teller Monica saw in New Orleans said the love of Monica's life would have a name starting with **P.** Monica doesn't have any more faith in fortune-tellers now than she did before the reading. But here's the thing: the day after she and Polly came back from their trip, Polly met a man at the Henhouse who kept an apartment in Paris. Just like her fortune-teller said she would. Astonishing that such a person would come into the Henhouse, but such a person did. He was a movie person, out on a cross-country trip, exploring the back roads in search of a location. Needed to be a really small town in the Midwest, which of course is exactly what Mason is. In the end, he decided not to pick Mason for the movie, but didn't he just pick Polly for someone to spend the evening with, and they got along like a house afire. Polly came into work the next day dreamy as an old-fashioned high school girl wearing bobby sox and a ribbon around her ponytail. The guy—his name was Larry Bristol— had asked Polly to finish his road trip with him. Oh, he'd take care of separate accommodations at night, she shouldn't worry about that, but he thought she'd be an awful lot of fun to have on the drive back out to L.A. And then he'd buy her an airline ticket home, if she wanted to go back home. "Would you be in charge while I'm gone?" Polly asked Monica. And Monica said sure.

"I'll pay you extra, of course," Polly said, and Monica said never mind, she didn't have to.

"Time and a half," said Polly, and Monica said all right.

Monica has never thought of herself as a jealous person, but she has begun to grind her teeth in the daytime as well as at night and nearly weep into the bowl of chicken dumpling soup she has for lunch every day at the Henhouse. Maybe she should switch up soups.

In fact, maybe she should switch up everything in her life.

Wait.

Maybe she should! Who's stopping her? Only her! Why, she could start to change her life right this very second!

"Two slabs, two wrecked, burned British, jam in the alley!" Roberto calls out, and Monica says, "Got it." Which she thinks might be prophetic.

She delivers the order and she's suddenly thinking a mile a minute about things to do: Go after what she wants like she deserves it. Think positive. Get a new haircut, drive over to Columbia—or even St. Louis!—and get a great new haircut. Buy some new makeup, buy a pair of those sexy hoop earrings. And next time she sees Tiny alone, ask him out again. Only this time, instead of thinking, **Oh, my goodness, I'm so nervous, he's going to say no, he's going to say no,** think **Say yes, you little cupcake. You know you want to. You say yes, right now.**

Buy new underwear. Buy fancy dish soap that smells as good as perfume. Go to the library and find books on . . . well, go to the self-help section and see what's there.

"Honey, you're fine just the way you are!" her mother used to tell her, especially after she'd suffered another breakup.

Well, no, she's not just fine the way she is. Obviously. But she's not going to be the calm center of a storm with everything around her swirling at a dizzying pace. She's going to jump out there and swirl, too.

And looky here. Look who just came in the door. Alone. Talk about the power of positive thinking.

Tiny moves to the counter and Monica motions to Janelle, who is the counter waitress, to come over. "Let's switch sections for a while," she says. Janelle is only too happy to oblige. So many of those counter people still think they can slide some change beneath the lip of a saucer and call it a tip.

Tiny lowers himself onto the stool and picks up a

menu. He doesn't see Monica gliding over, doesn't
see her until she is directly before him.

Then, "Oh, hey!" he says. "Hey, Monica. Gosh!"

"Hey, Tiny."

"How are you?"

"I'm fine. You?"

"Yeah! I'm okay!" He looks at the menu again,
then closes it. "Guess I'd better eat and go, I've got
to get to work."

"Sure. Double pigs in a blanket?"

"Well, no, actually. Not today. I'm kind of switch-
ing things up a bit."

**Serendipity!** Monica thinks. **Talk about a sign!**
He's practically hers. They're practically married and
lying in bed at night in their Sleep Number bed.
They'll get one of those, Monica has saved up enough
for one, but it seems weird to get one for one person.
It would be like going on a roller coaster ride alone.

"Monica?"

"Yes?"

"I need to order, so could you find Janelle?"

"I'll take your order."

"That's okay. I'll give it to Janelle. This is her section, right?"

"Usually, it is. But not today. Today, I'm your girl."
Look at that. Look how she did that.

"Well . . ." He looks at his watch. "Oh, jeez. You
know what? I guess I miscalculated. I've got to pick
someone up in just a couple of minutes. I'd better
just . . ."

He lays down a five-dollar bill and races out.

She watches him go. She guesses he's in a hurry, all right; looks like he forgot his belt, the way his pants are hanging on him.

"Janelle!" she calls.

The waitress comes over and Monica says, "Let's switch back."

"Aw, really? I hadn't even gotten started over there. Can't I keep it just for today? I'll get some good tips with lunch."

"All right," Monica says, and then, "Hey, you waited on Tiny, right, last few times he came in?"

"Yup. He's a good tipper. He only gets a boiled egg and dry toast, but he leaves me a few bucks anyhow."

"Boiled egg and dry **toast**?" Monica asks.

"Um-hm, and he didn't even put no cream or sugar in his coffee. Skim milk. That's it." She lowers her voice, steps in closer to Monica. "Do you think he's sick? Do you think he's got some horrible disease that—"

"No. I think he's on a diet."

"Lordy! **Tiny**? What would Tiny be on a diet for? He's one of those seems right stubborn 'bout his weight. I wonder what happened!"

**Iris,** Monica thinks. Iris happened. Iris with her beautiful blond hair and svelte figure and high cheekbones and her big-city sophistication.

Well, there you go. Polly is off on a wondrous adventure, having her fortune come true. Maybe she'll stay out there in L.A. and sell her café, that was another thing the fortune-teller told her would happen, she'd sell her café, and then it would fail and go out of business.

But maybe she'll sell the Henhouse to Monica, and rather than the café failing, Monica will make it an even bigger success. And then she can at least be a successful business owner and her love life won't matter so much. Who has time for a relationship, she'll say, like all those women she's read about in magazines. She'll serve breakfast all day, people love breakfast. She'll put some things on the menu that Polly never would: Sweet-potato fries. Deviled eggs with bacon garnish. Peanut butter and pickle sandwiches and deep-fried pickles, both of which Monica loves and which are surprisingly good. Veggie burgers. Polly always said if you want a burger, you don't want it made of vegetables, you want it made of cow. But Monica will add turkey burgers and veggie burgers. She'll put a fresh flower on every table, too, another thing Polly would never do.

Her spirits rise, and suddenly she's hungry.

**His name will start with a** P, my eye. On the way to the kitchen, Monica looks around the crowded café. If every guy in there had a name that started with a P, she wouldn't be interested in a single one of them. Not one.

Her mother about her father: **I'll tell you something, honey. I didn't even talk to him. I just saw him, and I knew. Now, I was engaged to another feller, and I couldn't get that ring off my finger fast enough. I hated being so mean, but I'd found the** one I thought I'd never find, and wasn't any swaying me from doing what I had to do. And I have never regretted it. That's what I want for you.

For the first time in her life, Monica is glad her mother is gone. Because she is giving up. She is trading love for money.

She goes back to the kitchen and says, "Dish me up some chili, would you, Roberto?"

"No chili today. Vegetable soup and chicken dumpling soup only."

"But I want chili."

"There is no chili."

She moves closer and crosses her arms. "Make some. I am the captain now."

Roberto laughs, salutes, and starts making chili. Monica goes out to make sure everyone at her station is taken care of. There's a man sitting at the end of the counter studying the menu, and Monica goes over to him.

"Good afternoon!" she says, and when he looks up at her she practically faints. There are the eyes of Paul Newman, reborn. There they are. And the rest of the guy is pretty great, too: Curly black hair. A cleft chin. Heavens!

"Do you know what you'd like?" she asks.

"First time here," he says. "Are you still serving breakfast?"

See? Monica thinks. **People want breakfast all the time.**

"We are," she says. **For you.**

"Okay. So would you recommend the Maple Sausage Sandwich or the Eggs Fiesta?"

"They're both good," Monica says.

"Come on now, you have a favorite."

"I do. But it's neither of those."

"What is it?"

"The Flapjack Kerfuffle. It's pancakes with bacon and maple syrup already mixed in. That's my favorite."

"Well, then, that's what I'll have. And coffee. And orange juice. And your phone number."

Monica smiles at him and goes back to the kitchen to place the order.

"It's lunchtime now," Roberto says, and Monica says, "Make it anyway. Hey, Roberto, what do you think about making breakfast available all day?"

He shrugs. "People seem to like it."

Monica goes into the corner of the kitchen to sit on a stool and wait, and when the order is ready, she rushes out to deliver it. Across the room, she sees Janelle standing frozen, looking at the man Monica has just served like, **Uff da!** which she says all the time because her grandmother was Norwegian. Monica would bet Janelle is wishing she had her usual station right about now. She raises her eyebrows at Janelle, and Janelle blows air out of her cheeks and lifts her uniform up and down from her chest.

By the time the man has finished eating, they've had a pleasant conversation. He's a truck driver, passes through this way quite often, though he's never been here before. But he'll be back now that he knows what a good place it is. He'll be back in two days, in fact, will Monica be here then?

"Yes, I will," she says.

He squints at her name tag. "And your name is . . . Monica?"

"Right."

He stands to take his wallet out.

Oh. He's short.

Well, that's all right. What difference does it make? Okay, it makes a little difference at first, but you could get used to it. Monica's not that much taller, maybe a few inches.

"I'm Phil," he says. "Phil Porter."

"Nice to meet you," Monica says faintly. **A double** P!!!

Phil pulls a card out of his wallet. "I know you don't want to give me your number, at least not yet. But here's mine. In case you get bored tonight and want to have a conversation."

Monica can't wait to get bored. She might take a bath tonight and put on her pretty blue nightie and pour herself a glass of wine and get bored as can be.

# Soft Ball

"WHERE'S LUCILLE?" MONICA ASKS, WHEN she shows up for her caramel cake class. Here in Lucille's kitchen is an awful sight: Iris Winters.

"Lucille woke up a little under the weather," Iris says. "So I'll be teaching the class today."

The two of them stand there looking at each other, but then the doorbell rings—a group of four women arriving. Already they're giggling and carrying on, excited to be here. But that's because of Lucille, who is so funny, sometimes without knowing it. And she's sweet to her students—strict, yes, even gruff, but kind. Monica guesses everyone will be disappointed to see Miss Uptight substituting. She'd heard that Lucille had hired an assistant, but, good Lord, couldn't she have found someone else? Monica knows Iris tries to be friendly, but it's just an act. Women as beautiful as Iris is never have to be really friendly; everything is just given to them. Also: they take whatever they want. Such as another woman's man.

But after a little moment of confusion, everyone but Monica seems to be okay with Iris teaching. Iris tells them Lucille is right upstairs, resting, and she expects to be fully recovered by tomorrow. She said she would check in at the end of the class to see if there were any questions, and to thank them for coming. "But for now," Iris says, "it's just me. As most of you know, I'm Lucille's assistant, Iris Winters. And today we're going to make a fantastic caramel cake. **After** we taste one."

From the counter behind her, she pulls out a picture-perfect caramel cake on a crystal cake pedestal, one slice missing, as always. Lucille not only tastes her demo cakes, she likes to show off how pretty the insides are. The perfect crumb. The evenness of the layers.

Each woman gets a little sample slice of cake on a pretty green depression-glass cake plate along with a cup of coffee, and every one of them proclaims the cake delicious, including Monica. Now let's just see if Iris can teach them how to make it.

Iris clears her throat. "Okay, so first, why don't you all pick out aprons?"

"We wear aprons?" asks Molly, the only woman who hasn't taken a class from Lucille before. To another woman, she says, in a low voice, "Who wears **aprons** anymore?"

"I've laid some out for you to choose from," Iris

says, pointing to the five bib aprons she has put in the corner of the kitchen. One has cherries on it. One red-and-white one has the cutest sweetheart neckline. One is festooned with yellow cabbage roses. One has three wide multicolored ruffles at the bottom and a big bow tied at the hip. One has flower pots for pockets, with embroidered flowers coming out of them. Iris herself is wearing an apron that features a map of Florida, lots of little figures wearing bikinis, eating oranges, swimming in the ocean.

There's an awkward moment when two of the women both want the cabbage rose apron but they work it out—they decide to switch aprons halfway through the class.

"Next," Iris says, "we'll assemble our ingredients."

She sounds more confident now, and Monica is disappointed. She does not wish Iris well.

Iris stresses the importance of beating the already-mixed butter and sugar for another five minutes after the four eggs have been added—one at a time, so that they mix better.

Monica raises her hand, feeling as if little devil horns have sprouted at the top of her head. "**Why** do the eggs mix better that way?"

"Why?" Iris asks. Stalling, obviously.

A few moments go by, and Iris looks panicked.

Finally, one of the other women turns around to look at Monica. "It's so they can emulsify with the fats," she says. "Which you know, Monica, because you were in class with me when Lucille told us that."

"Well, I forgot," Monica says, though she did not.

"I have a question," says Molly, the new woman. The look on Iris's face is deer-in-the-headlights.

"Why do you have to alternate adding the milk and the flour?"

"Oh, that's just to prevent overmixing," Iris says, grateful that she remembers Lucille recently answering this same question.

Then Monica raises her hand again. "I know this sounds kind of funny, but what does milk do in cakes?"

"What does it **do**?" Iris asks. Silence, and Monica crosses her arms and sits back in her chair.

**The devil came a-calling and sure enough found you home!** her mother would have said about Monica's behavior right now. And she's right. Worse than that, Monica is enjoying herself.

There is the sound of a toilet flushing upstairs, and then they hear Lucille calling down, "Milk has protein that creates a strong batter. It has to be strong so it can withstand the rigors of baking. The sugar and fat in milk help tenderize and moisten, and they also add flavor. Sugar also helps create a golden-brown crust. Any other questions, Monica?"

"No, ma'am," Monica says.

"What's that?"

"No, ma'am," she says, louder.

**Clomp, clomp, clomp,** the women hear. **Bang!** goes a door. Apparently, Lucille has gone back to bed.

When the cake is in the oven, Iris says, "Now we'll

make the frosting, and what we will learn here is how to determine if you have reached the soft-ball stage. If you have a candy thermometer, it's easy enough, you just check to see when the temperature has reached two hundred thirty-five, two hundred forty degrees. How many of you have a candy thermometer?"

Only one hand goes up.

"No worries, I don't have one, either," Iris says. "So I'll show you another way to tell. We'll use the cold-water test. You just drop a bit of the frosting into a cup of cold water, and if it's at the soft-ball stage, it will form a flexible ball. And then if you put it in your hand for just a few seconds, it will flatten out. I'll show you, you'll each get a chance to do it."

Monica doesn't want to do it. She wants to go home. She's ashamed of being called out for being a jerk, she's ashamed that she's trying to punish Iris for taking Tiny. When it's her turn, she drops her frosting in the cold water, then holds it in her hand, watching it flatten, all the while never making eye contact with Little Miss Brahmin. That's what Polly called her, Little Miss Brahmin. "What's Brahmin?" Monica asked, and Polly told her it was someone from the upper class in New England, and she also said that Brahmins had sticks up their you-know-whats, and Monica said, "Right," though of course she had no idea if that was so.

The cake Iris makes is absolutely delicious. Monica sighs hugely when she eats her full-size piece. Sally

Finder, the woman next to her and a regular at the Henhouse (chicken croquettes, extra gravy for lunch every time she comes), says to Monica, "Isn't it divine?"

"Yup," Monica says, though that is not why she was sighing. She was sighing because she was thinking about Iris making this cake for Tiny.

Sally says, "You should sell these cakes at the Henhouse. I'll bet Lucille would make them for you."

"That's a good idea," Monica says, and so at least one good thing has come from taking the class. She'll suggest it to Polly. Or, given the fact that she's in charge now, she'll ask Lucille herself. Might be good to wait a day or so, though.

When the class is over, Lucille makes a brief appearance to thank the women for coming. Her hair is sticking out all over her head and she looks half asleep, so when she asks if there are questions, no one asks her any.

But on the way out, Molly, the new woman, asks Iris, "Where did the aprons come from?"

"Lucille buys them at antiques stores," Iris says. "But this one I'm wearing I found on eBay. Do you like it?"

"I love it!" the woman says. "I just never wore aprons, but now I want to."

Iris unties the apron and gives it to the woman.

"Oh, no," she says. "I can't take that."

"Sure you can," Iris says. "I've got tons more. Lucille got me going on them."

Monica is the last one to leave. She has to do it. "Sorry I was so bitchy," she says.

"It's okay," Iris says. "It's good for me to get asked questions."

In her car, Monica thinks: **I have to move on. I have to get a life.**

# Heating Up in the Kitchen

———

At nine-thirty in the morning, Iris rings Lucille's doorbell.

"Use your key!" she hears Lucille call out.

She finds Lucille at the kitchen table, still in her nightgown.

"I'm still feeling a little punk," Lucille says. "But I'm better. Show me what you've got."

Iris reaches into her leather tote and pulls out a couple of folders. She has learned that Lucille will tolerate looking at a computer screen if she must, but she prefers a hands-on approach.

From one folder, Iris pulls out recipes she's found here and there: online, in newspapers, in her own cookbooks or in those at the library. The one she shows Lucille now came from a book in the library and is for a monkey cake. It's just the animal's head, but it's darling.

Lucille peers at the photo. "Huh. Isn't that cute! I wonder how they got the head so perfect."

Iris knows full well that Lucille knows the answer to that question, but she wants Iris to feel important. And so Iris says, "You bake it in a bowl."

"I see," Lucille says. "Well, add it to the kids' class curriculum, and we'll teach them how to make banana pudding with toasted coconut that day, too. I think we still have some jungle plates. What else do you have? Did you find some more ideas for men's classes?"

"I thought you'd never ask," Iris says, and pulls out a recipe she just found in the newspaper. "Beer and bacon muffins."

Lucille wrinkles her nose. "Do you think they'd be good?"

"I tried them. They're sensational."

"With bacon jam?"

"Perfect. And we'll add a cheese omelet? And virgin Bloody Marys?"

"I'm glad I hired you, Iris."

"I'm glad you did, too. Now give me your list. I'll order you whatever you need online, and then I'll go over to the fabric store to get the ribbon you want for the Thanksgiving class."

"See if there are any more good aprons at Time's Treasures, too. We might could use a couple more for men. Things are heating up with them."

# Abby and Lincoln

―――

Abby asks Lincoln to wait in the lounge by the nurses' station for just a minute. She wants to talk to Dad alone.

"Why?" he asks.

"It's private," she says. And then, seeing the fear in his face, "It's about your birthday. Only two weeks away! And that's all I'm saying."

He stands there, and she has the feeling he wants to say he doesn't care about his birthday, but thinks maybe it would hurt her feelings if he did. He offers a quick smile and heads out to the lounge. He'll do his homework there, and no doubt one of the nurses will bring him ice cream or some other treat that they keep on hand for the patients.

"The nurses really like him," Abby says, after Lincoln leaves the room.

Jason smiles. "Everybody likes him. He's Lincoln."

She leans back against her pillow. "Can you lower me a bit, sweetheart?"

He presses the button to get her to the forty-five degree angle she prefers. "Okay?"

She nods.

"Jason, will you make a party for him?"

"Sure, but I don't think he wants one. I think he wants to wait until you come home."

"I know. . . ." She shrugs. "Okay, I don't want to say this, but . . ." She reaches out to cover his hand with her own and whispers. "I don't think I'm coming home."

"Yes you are," Jason says. "You're just having a bad day. You've had this happen before, and then the next day you're fine."

"Well. Not **fine.**"

"Better, then."

"You think that's what's happening? You don't think I'm dying?" She'll trust whatever he says. He knows her better than the cadre of doctors who surround her every morning. He knows her better than the hospitalist, who keeps saying, "I wish I had better news."

Jason leans in close to her. "I think you'll go into remission and you'll get to come home."

"Okay."

"Are you beat, sweetheart? You want me to go?"

"Maybe. But will you read to me first? Will you read me to sleep? What are you reading?"

"Oh, it's interesting. It's a book about time. About the relativity of time. And the writing is so . . .

poetic. It talks about how we're not so very good at understanding time, it's far more complex than we thought. It turns out that physical time really does run at different speeds."

"Huh!" Abby says, and for one moment, she is herself again, lifted away from everything else by the ideas that a book can suggest. But these concepts are too difficult for her right now. They slip away from her when she tries to think about them. "That is interesting," she tells Jason, and she is disappointed to feel that she is falling asleep again. This is what she does. She sleeps or hurts. Or she stares at things with a level of incomprehension or confusion that frightens her. Yesterday she studied a rose in the bouquet by her bed for the longest time, trying to understand what red was. When the nurse came in, Abby pointed and said, "What is that color on that flower?" The nurse said, "I guess I would call it cardinal red." And Abby seemed to come to, then, seemed to jump back into her brain. "That's a good word for it," she said.

"Maybe read to me next time, okay?" she tells Jason now, and closes her eyes. Merciful. Merciful. Her lids seem to sink down into her eye sockets.

He bends to kiss her forehead, her mouth. "I love you so much."

"Me, too, you," she says. And then, opening her eyes, "Don't forget. Ask Linky if he wants a party."

"**Link,** if you please."

She smiles. "Oh, yeah. Right."

"I'll talk to him about it on the way home."

"Okay. You want to bring him back in now so I can say goodbye?"

"Sure." He stands, gives her a kind of appraising look, then says, gently, "Sweetheart? Do you want to . . . Should I put a little lipstick on you?"

She puts her hand to her mouth. "Oh! Oh, yes, that would be good, I forgot. I know, I'm awfully pale, aren't I? There's pink lip gloss in the top drawer there. Can you give it to me?"

He digs around and holds up a tube. "This one?"

"Yeah." She uncaps the lipstick and puts it to her mouth. Her hand is shaking.

"Want me to do it?" Jason asks.

"I can." She forgot to ask for a mirror, but never mind.

Jason leaves the room to go and get Lincoln. Thinking of her son, Abby can feel her heart seem to stretch. It hurts. When he walks in, she rouses every bit of energy she has in order to hold out her arms and look glad. Lincoln walks slowly to her, she who is no longer she, but whom he loves, and she folds him into her.

"Bye, Mom," he says, his voice a bit muffled.

"You go to the shelter and get a kitty, okay?" she says. "That will be your birthday present from me."

"Okay."

"Great!" she says, but after he goes out the door, she screws up her face and silently weeps.

# Cookies and Kittens

===

THREE DAYS BEFORE THANKSGIVING, LUCILLE and Iris are frosting the wattles on the turkey cookies they have made as a demo for the baking class tomorrow. "A Turkey of a Hostess Gift," Lucille had decided to call this class. "Um," Iris said. "Are you sure you want to call it that? A turkey of a gift would mean—"

"It's a joke!" Lucille said, and so Iris simply wrote a description online that suggested you'd likely be canonized if you brought these cookies to whomever was having you for the holiday. Lucille got quite a response. Tomorrow, fifteen women will be there to make cookies, box them up in cute little corrugated boxes, and tie on brown-and-orange-plaid ribbon. Iris found the boxes at a dollar store, and Lucille told her, "I'm thrilled that everything was so cheap. You have a real gift." She hasn't praised Iris's baking skills that highly. Yet.

While the cookies baked, they set up the kitchen for the class. They put extra leaves in the kitchen table and arranged chairs as best they could. "It looks like the White House briefing room in here," Lucille grumbled.

But Iris thought she was pleased. Last week, Iris had to buy six more folding chairs, and Lucille said they might need to get a few more yet.

"I think I might get business cards that say LUCILLE HOWARD, BAKER TO THE STARS," Lucille says now.

"What stars?" Iris asks.

"You know, movie stars."

"You bake for movie stars?"

"Well, not yet, but it's not impossible."

"Maybe not, but you should probably have had some dealings with movie stars before you put that on your card."

Lucille sighs. "Stop being so technical. Tell me this: If movie stars ate my baking, wouldn't they like it?"

"No doubt. Those who eat sweets, anyway."

Lucille waves her hand. "They all eat sweets. Whether they admit it or not."

"Some people don't even like sweets."

**"Who?"**

"My ex-husband, for one." She attempted to write to him again just last night. Here's how far she got: **Dear Ed, I suppose it might be too late to say this.**

Then yet another card ripped up, this one with a beautiful waterfall on it.

"Your ex is a bit of an anomaly, I think you would agree. And anyway, what's to **stop** me from sending some things to movie stars through their agents? I might send some blondies to Nicole Kidman, I think she's exactly the type for blondies."

"Well, but . . . I think they'd get thrown out," Iris ventures.

"What's that?"

"I said I think they'd get thrown out."

Lucille pulls her chin in and blinks once, twice.

"Why in the world would they throw them out?"

"For safety reasons," Iris says. "Famous people can't eat what just anyone sends them."

Lucille shakes her head. "It's a sad world, I'll tell you. But there's nothing saying I couldn't send to a few, anyway. And then say I am baker to the stars. They might not eat it, but I can bake for them."

Iris leans forward. "Lucille? You don't need to do that. **You're** the star, at least in this town. Everyone knows about your baking."

"I suppose it's true."

Lucille leans back and squints at the cookie she holds up before her. "Not red enough."

"Let's see," Iris says, and then, "Yeah, you're right. Want me to mix up some buttercream and we can add more food coloring this time?"

Lucille looks up at her cuckoo clock: just after eight. "I don't think so. Maybe I'll quick make it tomorrow before they come."

"I can do it at home," Iris says. "I'll bring it over tomorrow when I come. And I'll get some more food coloring, you're running low."

"Only organic!" Lucille says, and Iris says, "I **know**."

"Do not deviate one bit from my recipe, either."

"Would I do that?"

Lucille pushes herself up from the table and Iris has to keep herself from helping. Lucille does not like you to help her. But Iris can see she is tired.

"Anything else I can do for you?" she asks.

Lucille puts her hands on her hips and narrows her eyes as she surveys the kitchen. "No, if we get that color right, we're all set. I'll see you in the morning. I'd better use the thirty-six-cup coffeemaker for this crowd!"

"I'll come early and get the coffee started. That big one takes a good forty-five minutes to brew."

Lucille hesitates, and then says thank you, and suddenly Iris is worried. Lucille gave in too easily. She usually puts up more of a fight, saying things like "Do I look helpless?" or "Here comes your age-ism, creeping in again."

In addition to running her classes and making caramel cakes for the Henhouse, Iris knows Lucille has been taking care of the boy next door quite a bit. She says he's a sweet kid and not really any trouble. He comes after school and stays until his dad gets home at dinnertime, having spent most of the day with his wife. She's at the regional hospital in Columbia undergoing some experimental treatment,

Lucille said, and apparently is not doing well. Link has a snack, does his homework, and then helps Lucille prepare demos. He likes cooking, apparently; Lucille said he wields a rubber spatula with some flair. She said sometimes he goes to a friend's house instead of coming to Lucille's, but lately he's there every day. Lucille says she thinks he's scared.

Yesterday, Lucille asked Iris to take Link to the animal shelter. His parents agreed to let him have a kitten, and so he and Iris went to see what was available.

A lot was available, as it happened. Three new litters had just been brought in, and Iris had to bite her tongue in order not to make any recommendations. There were orange ones, tabbies, and ones that looked a little Siamese. Link sat with one kitten in his lap, then another, and more after that, but couldn't make up his mind. Finally, Iris said, "How about if I bring you back tomorrow?"

"I can't tomorrow. There's teachers' conferences at school, and my dad is bringing me to visit my mom."

"Oh, good," Iris said, and then wondered if it was crass to say that it was good when you had to visit your mother in the hospital. She quickly added, "Why don't you take some pictures of the ones you like best, and you can show her. Okay?"

He smiled, nodded, and then picked out his three favorites and photographed them. "This one here is Slinky," he said of a gray tabby, the only one he named, and Iris thought, **There's your kitten.** But Link had to be the one to say it. And he didn't.

Iris had found her own kitten, though, and she brought him home. He's orange, with blue eyes and a patch on his chest like a heart. She named him Homer. For home. Which is what she believes she has found here. The regret she anguishes over has not left her. But more things are accumulating between her and it.

When she pulls into the parking lot of her apartment building, she sees Tiny climbing out of his truck. She calls his name, then starts over to him. "What are you up to?"

"Just going for my walk by the river. Want to come?"

"Sure!"

They walk quietly for a while, Tiny going at a much faster pace than he used to.

"You're looking good, Tiny," she tells him. "You've lost a lot of weight."

"Thanks. But I sure miss my pigs in a blanket."

"You'll have them again."

"Probably not the double order, though."

"You might not want the double order anymore."

Tiny stops in his tracks and turns to face her. "Iris, I will want a double order of pigs in a blanket every day probably for the rest of my life. Some men want a big bank account so they feel rich. Me, if I look down at a platter and see it covered with cakes and sausage and maple syrup, I'm good. You know? I'm great."

They start walking again. It's a bit cold, but energizing.

She hears Tiny sigh, and when she looks over, his face is drooping, sad.

"Tiny? Are you . . . is something wrong?"

"Nah. Nothing I want to talk about. Best get back, huh?"

When they reach their building, Iris says, "Listen, I'm going to make some things for Lucille's class tomorrow and then I'm going to find a funny movie on demand. Want to come over and watch with me?"

"That sounds nice, but I have to do a real early morning pickup tomorrow to take a guy to the airport. Four-thirty A.M."

"Ouch!"

"Yeah, but you know. Buys the Lean Cuisines."

"Okay, another time."

They stand quietly at the elevator door and then Iris says, "You know, Tiny, I have a Weight Watchers cookbook, and there's a recipe in there that is so low-calorie. You know what it's for?"

"What?"

"Chicken and dumplings."

"Can't be."

"It is! It's six points."

"I don't know what that means."

"It means it's low-cal, low-fat," Iris says. I'll make it for you tomorrow."

"That's okay. But thanks."

The elevator comes, and they step in. "You sure you're okay?" Iris asks.

He stares at the floor. "Well, I finally asked Monica

Mayhew out today." He looks over at Iris. "You know what she said? She said no."

Iris is speechless. Finally, she says, **"Why?"**

Tiny shrugs. "Don't know, really. She said thanks, but she's moved on. I hate that, 'moved on,' when it means you're being left behind. It's the loneliest, most awful feeling. I been sitting in my truck trying to think what happened. I guess she's probably found someone else. Seems like I've lost her and Dan, too. I found out today that he moved. He moved and he didn't even tell me. After Monica said no, I went over to see him. I thought maybe if I just surprised him, we could talk. But he's gone. His neighbor said he moved to Chicago. He didn't say a word to me. I thought I was his best friend. I'd come to think maybe Monica cared for me. I don't know. I guess I just don't know. I got to think about all this, you know?" When the doors open, he says, "I'll see you later," and moves slowly down the hall to his apartment.

Iris lets herself in and is met at the door by Homer, mewing. "I know," she says. "I know."

# Off the Wagon

═══

TINY UNLOADS ONTO THE DINING ROOM TABLE what he's brought home for dinner: a Double Whopper, heavy everything. Large fries, large onion rings. After he eats this, he'll go over to Willigan's and get the turtle sundae.

He sits down and takes a huge bite of the Whopper. "That's what I'm talking about," he says to no one. To no one.

He stops chewing. Lifts his eyes to look out the window. There's the great outdoors. Out there are people he's never met. There are things going on that might be interesting to see.

A one-woman man. Stupid! He's stupid to feel that way.

Dan was right; women do like him. Unaccountably, perhaps, but they like him. He can go out there and find another one. Monica doesn't have such a hold on him that he can't go out looking. He'll head over to the Alarm Bell and see what's up. See if that red-head is there.

He looks down at the Whopper in his hand, which he is barely keeping together. He looks at the rest of the food he's brought home and suddenly leaps up, gathers all the food together, and throws it out. A sin, at least a venial sin, but there it is, he's done it. Losing weight is something that he was doing for himself, too, not just for Monica.

He puts on his jacket, checks to see that he has his phone. Opens the door, then closes it without going out.

He hangs up his coat and goes back into the kitchen. On top of the trash are the onion rings, still wrapped up. He takes one out and eats it, and then he goes to bed. Seven o'clock.

# A Good Talking-to

=

AFTER THE THANKSGIVING COOKIE CLASS—
a resounding success—Lucille asks Iris if she
would mind taking a caramel cake over to the Henhouse. It's only one cake this time—Lucille couldn't
quite manage to make more—but they'll be thrilled
to have it, she says. Most popular thing on the menu,
she says.

"I'll be glad to," Iris says. She welcomes the opportunity to have a word with Monica.

There are only a few cars in the parking lot when
she gets to the Henhouse. It's the dead hour, between
lunch and dinner. She sits at the table Tiny usually
sits at, so that Monica will wait on her. But Monica
and another waitress are sitting together at a corner
table, and it's not Monica who comes over, it's
the other one, the one with the beehive and puffy
bangs.

"Hey there," the waitress—Iris sees her name is Janelle—says. "What can I do you for?"

"Just the grilled cheese," Iris says. "And an iced tea. And I have a caramel cake here for you, too, from Lucille."

"Oh, good. We can't get enough of it, it's the most popular thing on the menu."

"So she said."

"Lucille usually brings it in herself."

"I know, but she asked me to bring it today." She slides over the pink bakery box, LUCILLE HOWARD in embossed gold across the top. It was Iris's idea to create these boxes, and she talked Lucille into spending the money on them because she said it would be excellent advertising. After lengthy consultation with Iris, who showed Lucille page after page of fonts on the computer, Lucille chose a flowing, flowery script that Iris thinks is really quite pretty. She wanted to put floating cookies and cakes on the box, too, but when Iris told her how much more it would be, she said imagination was better anyway.

"We usually get two cakes," Janelle says suspiciously, and Iris begins to think Janelle doesn't like her any more than Monica does.

"Lucille's awfully busy, so it's only one today," Iris says. "I'm Iris Winters, by the way, I'm Lucille's assistant."

"I know your name. Your first one, anyway."

"Oh! Well, it's nice to meet you."

"I'll get your sandwich right out." Janelle snatches up the cake and makes her way to the kitchen.

Monica is reading the paper and eating from a platter of French fries that the women are evidently sharing. The café is empty enough that when Iris says, "Monica?" she's sure she can hear her. But maybe not, because she doesn't look up.

"Monica!" a man at a table close by her says.

She looks up.

The man, an older gent in bib jeans, a T-shirt, a jean jacket, and a feed-store cap, gestures over to Iris. "Lady over there's calling you."

Monica looks at Iris, sighs, and comes over.

"Could I talk to you?" Iris says.

"I'm right here."

"I'd like to talk to you about Tiny."

Monica sits down, her arms crossed. "What."

"As I think you know, Tiny and I are friends."

"Yeah, pretty good friends, it seems to me."

"Oh, we're not . . . Did you think . . . ? We're just friends!"

Monica shrugs. "So what about him?"

"I hope it's not wrong for me to do this, but I wanted to let you know that he really cares for you."

Now Monica's face changes, it softens, and she looks down at the table to say, "Well, he sure has a funny way of showing it."

"He's awfully shy. How about we have dinner one night and talk?"

The door opens and a man walks in. Both of the women turn to look at him. **Wow, look at those eyes**, Iris thinks.

"Ready?" he asks Monica, and she leaps to her feet.

"I gotta go," she tells Iris. And to the man, "Hey, Phil. Just getting my purse. Be right there, hon."

**Damn it,** Iris thinks.

She watches as Monica gets into the man's truck—a tractor trailer cab, and the man has to really boost Monica up to get her into the seat. Then he climbs into his side and reaches over to kiss Monica. And Iris thinks, **Nope.** Monica doesn't lean in. She doesn't smile afterward. Instead, as they pull out of the parking lot, she looks back at Iris like Iris is the last puppy in the window. And Iris nods, in a kind of urgent way. Whatever that means. But she has to do something.

Janelle slaps her grilled cheese in front of her. "She's engaged, you know. He ain't got her the ring yet, but she's engaged."

# True Colors

——

"I JUST DON'T LIKE IT LIKE THAT, I TOLD YOU," PHIL tells Monica. They're having dinner at her house, and he has barely touched the steak she served him.

"It's medium rare, that's what you like."

He lifts the steak up with his knife and peers beneath it.

"This isn't medium rare, this is medium. I don't like it like that."

"Sorry," she says. That steak cost an arm and a leg. "Do you like the stuffed baked potato? Or the broccoli?"

"Hard to ruin that, isn't it?"

She doesn't answer.

"Hey," he says, his tone softening. "Don't get your little feelings hurt. C'mere." He pats his lap. Then, when she doesn't move, "**Mon**ica. Come here!"

She comes over to him and he pulls her down on

his lap and kisses her and her insides feel like they're sliding down to her toes. "Are you my girl?"

"Yes."

He runs his hand up her leg. Lord. The man knows what he's doing.

"How about we go to bed?"

"I . . . You don't want to finish dinner? Or eat dessert? I made a caramel cake."

"Is that cake going somewhere? Or do you think it might still be here till we're done? I've missed you, baby. That was a long trip."

He kisses her again, then kind of pushes her off his lap. "Let's go."

They go into her bedroom, where the sheets are freshly laundered in an expensive detergent and where there is a small bouquet on her nightstand and a newly placed, framed photo of the two of them that she had wanted to surprise him with. They're at an amusement park, where Monica asked someone to take their picture. They're hoisting up big cones of cotton candy, grinning. Happy.

He doesn't notice the photo and she thinks it would be better to show him later.

After they have undressed and are facing each other in bed, he pushes her hair back from her forehead and says again, "**Are** you my girl?"

"Yes, I am. 'Course I am." His erection is bothering Monica, banging up against her leg that way as though it's knocking.

"I could eat you up," he says, grinning. And he turns out the light.

Afterward, he closes his eyes.

"Phil?" she whispers. "Do you want dessert?" She herself is still really hungry; she didn't finish eating her dinner.

"I'm really tired. And we don't either of us need dessert."

She lies still until he starts snoring and then she goes into the dining room and finishes her dinner. After that, she cuts a huge piece of caramel cake and plops it onto a plate. She has almost finished eating it when Phil appears in his bathrobe. "I'm sorry. I'll eat now." He looks at her plate. "Oh. Wow. You ate that cake?"

# Hello?

———

IRIS IS LYING IN BED READING A RECIPE FOR banana-split cake in a cookbook for children when her cellphone rings. She looks at the clock: 10 P.M. So it isn't Lucille. She picks up her phone, checks the number on caller ID, and doesn't recognize it. Sales call? But they don't usually call late at night. She answers tentatively. "Hello?"

Silence.

**"Hello?"**

Nothing. Iris hangs up. She hates when that happens. It's like the beginning of a horror movie. Woman lying in bed innocently reading when her phone rings . . .

She's about to turn out the light and try to go to sleep when her phone rings again.

She answers gruffly, saying, "What." Right. That will show the psychopath what he's up against!

"It's me," a woman says. "Monica Mayhew. Sorry."

"Oh! Hello, Monica."

"I got your number from Lucille's website. I hope you don't mind my calling you."

"Not at all."

"That was me, who just hung up."

"Yes, I figured."

"I'm just calling . . . Okay. I'm calling to talk about Tiny. About what you said, that he cares for me."

"Oh, he does, he really does."

"Well . . . What does he say about me? I mean, you know, like . . . What does he **say**?"

Now Iris isn't sure what to do. It feels like it would be a betrayal to tell Monica the things Tiny told her in confidence.

"Hello?" Monica says.

"I guess all I can say is that, in **friendly** conversation, he has said things that make me know he cares for you. Why don't you call him?"

"I can't call him!"

"Why not?"

An exasperated sigh. "I can't call him and say, 'Are you in love with me?'"

"No, but you could just call and say . . . You could say . . ."

"See?" Monica says.

"Well, why don't you just ask him out?"

"I tried that."

"I'm pretty sure he'd say yes this time."

"I don't know," Monica says. "I would have to

hide it from Phil. And then, what if . . . I feel like if I'm going to ask Tiny out, I have to dump Phil first. Which I have never done, dumped a man. I'm not asking you what to do, but what do you think I should do?"

"I think we should meet for dinner tomorrow night. Can you? Maybe at Mama Mia's?"

"What time?"

"Six?" People eat awfully early here, that Iris has learned. Not only that, she has learned to like it.

"Okay. I'll see you there. And thanks, Iris."

"You're welcome."

Iris hangs up. She's glad she and Monica seem to be becoming friends. But she's sad to be reminded of the fact that she **has** dumped a man.

She didn't have to leave him in the way she did. There had been love between them.


THE NEXT EVENING, AFTER Monica and Iris have finished dinner, Monica says, "Hey. I need to go to the mall. I need to get some new lipstick. Something Tiny might like. Would you come with me?"

"Absolutely."

Half an hour later, at the cosmetics counter, Monica applies a shade of pink and turns to show Iris.

"Hmmm," Iris says. She takes a step back, crosses her arms, and tilts her head. Squints a bit. "It's okay, but let's try something else." She selects a red color and puts it on Monica herself. "Okay, look," she says, and when Monica turns to the mirror she nearly gasps.

"It looks great on you, right?" Iris says. "Look how it brings out your hair and your beautiful porcelain skin. Now smile and see how white your teeth look."

Monica smiles, and a fizz of pleasure runs through her. "Gosh! I never got red before because it always looked awful."

"Well, there's orange red and then there's blue red. This is a blue red. You're a winter, so that's what looks good on you."

"I'm a what?"

"A winter. Didn't you ever have your colors done?"

Monica shakes her head no. "I'm not too smart about fashion. I guess I'll always be one of those people who like kittens on clothes. And rhinestones. And I'm sorry, I know I'm a big girl, but I like to wear horizontal stripes!"

"You can wear horizontal stripes," Iris says. "They can actually be slimming. Don't listen to all those myths: no horizontal stripes, you're too old to wear something, all that. What **is** true is that proper fit is important, and that the colors you wear should flatter your skin tone and hair color. And you are a winter! That means you look good in very clear, almost sharp colors. You know, white and red and navy blue and black, you'd look fabulous in black, Monica, with some big silver hoop earrings. A really hot pink would be great on you, too. What you want to stay away from are subdued tones, like beige, which would yellow you out. In pastels, go for icy tones."

"How do you know all this?"

Iris shrugs. "I learned a lot when I had my consignment shop. I used to bring someone in to do colors for my customers."

Monica can hardly breathe. On the way into the store, she saw a dress on a mannequin that she loved. It had a skirt that would twirl. The fabric was so soft and it draped beautifully. But it was hot pink. That's what she had thought then: **But it's hot pink!**

"Iris," she says, "would you mind looking at a dress with me?"

# Pentimento

---

Lucille and Nola are out on the porch waiting for the snickerdoodles to cool. Maddy has gone with her fiancé to a photography exhibit in Columbia, and Lucille is babysitting until this evening. It's an unusually warm day; one hardly needs a sweater. Lucille would like Nola to take a nap, because she herself is tired. So far, nothing doing. Nola is on the porch swing, lying down, as Lucille requested, but wide awake.

"Can you see wind?" Nola asks. "Is it blue?"

"You can't see it, but you can see what it's doing," Lucille tells her. "Why don't you close your eyes for just a bit and see what happens?"

"But how can you see what it's doing if you can't see it?"

Lucille gestures from her rocker toward the trees lining the street. "See the tree branches moving?"

Nola points. "You mean there?"

"I mean everywhere."

"I can't see everywhere," Nola says.

"Okay, smartie, so look at that tree right there in front of us, see how it's moving?"

"Yes."

"Well, that's how you see wind. You see it moving the trees, or the grass, or you see it making ripples on the water or blowing your hair. You see the **effect** of the wind."

"Well, I want to see the **wind**."

"Too bad for you."

Nola considers this. "It's not too bad for me because I will make a way to see the wind because I will dye it blue."

"You do that." Lucille yawns. "And now how about you go to sleep for a bit?"

"I'm not sleepy."

"I am."

Nola hops off the swing. "Lie down here, Grandma."

Lucille rocks in her chair. It is tempting.

"Lie down, and I will watch over you."

The words bring sudden tears to Lucille's eyes and she wipes them away, embarrassed. That's what Frank did, made her feel watched over. It was the only time in her life she felt that way. All the rest of the time, it was Lucille watching out for Lucille. Oh, she could do it, but how nice it was for that brief period of time to feel like someone had her back, whether he was right with her or not. If he was in the world, he was watching over her.

Nola comes closer, puts her hands on Lucille's knees, and peers into her face. "Are you crying?"

"No."

"Uh-huh, yes you are. I see the tear buds."

Lucille gets up out of the rocker, and, with considerable effort, lies down on the swing. "There. I'm in the swing, just like you said. Now you watch over me."

"Okay." Nola covers her with the flannel quilt Lucille brought out to cover the child. Then she sits on the floor, and in a tiny voice begins to sing some sort of made-up, nonsense song. **"And when you sleeeeeep, I will be right heeeeere, I will be the ooooone who takes caaaaare of yoooooooooou!"** This last note is so high Lucille's eyes widen and she has to laugh.

"You sound like knives being sharpened," she tells Nola.

"Close your eyes, Grandma," Nola says, and Lucille does. She must not fall asleep, but oh, to be caught like that—that's how it feels, as if she is caught in a kind of golden cocoon. Never underestimate the joy of being the one who is cared for, is what Lucille thinks.

"I could comb your hair," Nola says.

"That would be lovely," Lucille tells her. And so Nola goes and gets her doll's hairbrush and she combs Lucille's hair gently and it feels so good Lucille thinks she ought to pay her.

———

After Maddy and Matthew come to collect Nola and leave their gifts of chicken chow mein for Lucille's dinner, and postcards of the photographs they saw (**The things people photograph these days—mounds of unrecognizable flesh!**), Lucille goes up to her bedroom. She takes off her shoes, rolls off her knee-high nylons. She unbuttons her house-dress at the waist, lies flat on her bed, and locks her hands over her belly. It's too late to nap, but oh, my, she needs a rest.

She looks around her bedroom. The walls are pink, Bakery Box Pink, it's called, a color she requested when she moved in with Arthur and Maddy. And Arthur said, **Why, sure,** which is pretty much how that man answered every request.

She hopes Arthur is with Nola, the wife he loved so dearly. Lucille does believe people see one another again, and she believes that pets will be reunited with their owners, too, though this is mostly acquiescence to those who cannot for one minute stop yammering on about their little fur babies, as they call them. Even if it turns out not to be true, what's the harm in believing it? It can bring some comfort.

She gets up onto her elbows and wiggles her toes. What a pleasure, to wiggle one's toes. She used to have pretty feet, but now her toes look like they can't agree on what direction they should go. Arthritis. She's deeply ashamed of her feet now. Whenever she has to go to the doctor, she tries to skip over the feet part. They're awful-looking, all lumpy and bumpy. Yet suddenly she feels a great affection for them.

Life is funny, isn't it? Funny in the way you can never predict not only what will happen, but who you'll become. Here she is, at the end of her life, and look what has happened. Who would have thought she'd become such a softie? Some creaky old gate opened when she met Frank, and now she is absolutely besotted with little Nola. She has developed a great warmth toward Iris, too, and even toward some members of her baking classes. No. Not just warmth, love. Look at that. One love departed, and all this followed. Seasons of the heart, she supposes. Never think winter will last when spring is equally inevitable.

When she taught fourth grade, there was one day when they deviated from fractions to talking about where people come from, because of a question a little girl asked. Normally, Lucille would not have tolerated such diversion, but it was one of those heartbreakingly beautiful fall days with a kind of benevolence in the air. And anyway, what the child asked had been interesting. Lucille still remembers little Peggy Sorenson, in her plaid dress and red cardigan sweater, raising her hand to say, "Miss Howard, is it true that people get born because God puts His thumb on their foreheads and pushes them down to earth?" There was a stunned silence, and before Lucille could ask what that had to do with fractions, another child said, "No, you dope, babies come from their mothers' tummies."

"But God put them in the moms' tummies," Peggy said, and then all the children began giggling and talking at once. Lucille calmed them down and told them there were different ideas about evolution, with some people believing that man was created by God and others believing people descended from the same ancestors as monkeys, and someday in science class, they would talk about all that, but for now, if she had a pie and wanted to cut it into fourths, how would she do that?

Well, it is a perpetual mystery, isn't it: evolution, the Big Bang, what caused what. Life is a mystery, death is a mystery, and everything in between is a mystery, too. The main thing is, people who are here, are here, for their own unique time upon the earth. She is one of the lucky ones, someone who has gotten to live a comfortable life up until this rather advanced age. She has not been the most graceful of her species. She has been clumsy in body and in spirit. She recalls a woman she once saw trying to maneuver around the washing machines on a Sears display floor. She was an overweight woman in a thin flowered dress and a tan coat, her banged-up purse hanging from the crook of her arm. She kept getting stuck between the machines, but her response to that was only to laugh, and she had the most beautiful, bell-like laugh, and the most beautiful smile, and she made the people around her smile with her. And now that Lucille is near the end, she holds that woman up as someone she aspires to be. Lucille is overly direct, and there is no changing that now. She is overly critical: ditto. But her heart has opened.

She takes in a big, bumpy breath. And then she begins to sing in a high little voice like Nola's, another nonsense song. **"Oh, I am heeeeere, I am right here,"** she sings, and then there is a catch in her throat and she stops singing. Everything is not such a mystery. She is not alone, and she never has been. Young or old, awake or in dreams, you see the effect of the wind.

# Pinwheels

—

LINCOLN IS AT LUCILLE'S FOR A SLEEPOVER. Jason is staying at the hospital tonight; he told Lucille they're trying one last experimental treatment on Abby. Apparently the side effects are pretty rough, though he didn't tell Lincoln that. He just said he'd like to spend the night with Mommy, and Lincoln was agreeable to staying with Lucille. He brought his new puppy with him.

"I thought you were getting a kitten!" Lucille says, eyeing the puppy as though the animal were black mold between her bathroom tiles. The dog is running around the kitchen, her tail wagging in circles like a propeller. Lucille prefers Henry, their older dog, who lay down in a corner of the living room after he arrived and hasn't budged since.

"Slinky? He got adopted. And then Iris took me to look at dogs and I found her and we called my parents and they said it would be okay. All Henry does is sleep."

Lucille thinks his parents would okay Lincoln adopting a rhinoceros if it would bring him comfort at this difficult time.

"Well," she says, "bring her upstairs and I'll sew her a diaper."

"She doesn't need that! She's already pretty much completely trained!"

But as if on cue, the dog urinates on the floor.

"Put her in the crate, put her in the crate!" Lucille says.

"She has to go **out**," Link says, scooping up the puppy. "I've got to take her **out** whenever she does that!"

"Well . . . Well . . . put your boots on! It's snowing out there! It's cold!"

Link slides into his boots and runs out into Lucille's backyard. The child has neglected to zip up his coat, and he stands there shivering, watching as the puppy sniffs everything in sight. Lucille has to admit the puppy is awfully cute, a kind of cocker with a face made for a greeting card. A sweet nature, too. However . . . She looks at the puddle of pee, then goes to get paper towels and bleach. Link will tell her he would have taken care of it, and he would have, would have done a good job, too, but she can't let it just sit there.

By the time Lincoln brings the dog in, Lucille has finished cleaning up, and, as predicted, Link starts to protest that he would have done it. But Lucille says, "It's just this once. If she pees again, it's all yours."

"She won't," Lincoln says. "She's just mixed up, being in a new place. She'll settle down."

They decide to make Christmas cookies, and Lucille shows the boy how to make pinwheels, and doesn't he think those are fun. She watches how carefully he places the rectangle of chocolate dough on top of the vanilla, and then she shows him how to roll everything up, jelly-roll style. They put the log of dough in the refrigerator until later that evening, when they can slice off the cookies to bake.

After a dinner of fish sticks and Tater Tots and candied carrots, they are sitting at the dining room table playing Crazy Eights and sampling the first batch of cookies out of the oven when Lincoln says, "Lucille? Why do you eat so much crap?"

She sits back in her chair. She gestures to the cookies. "You call this crap?"

"Yeah. I mean, they taste good, and they're pretty, but they're really bad for you."

"Oh, they are not."

"They have so much sugar! And butter!"

"Butter is good for you!"

"No it isn't."

She stands and rips off her apron. "Where's your phone?"

"In my backpack."

"Go and get it." These kids today. **Nola** knows how to look things up on a phone!

When Link returns, his phone in his hand, she says, "Ask it, 'Is butter good for you?'"

The boy talks into his phone, saying, "Hey Siri, is butter good for you?"

"Here's what I found on the Web," says some dis-embodied, suspiciously polite voice. Link reads silently, then says, "Wow. There's no association at all between saturated fat and cardiac disease. And here's an article on seven reasons why butter is **healthy** in moderation. But, uh-oh, there's also one called 'Can Butter Kill You?'"

"Give me that phone," Lucille says, lunging for it.

Lincoln laughs and pulls it away. He taps the screen, reads quickly. "Huh! Butter can't kill you, but margarine might! Wow!"

"Told you." Lucille goes into the kitchen to take the last batch of cookies from the oven, and Lincoln follows her.

"Wait till I tell my mom this," he says, and sud-denly the mood in the kitchen changes.

"How is your mom?" Lucille asks carefully. She puts the tray of cookies on top of the oven, turns it off.

"Bad."

She turns to look at the boy. "Oh, now."

"It's true. And you know it, too."

Lucille can't think of anything to say. Finally she manages, "I think you'd better let the puppy out once more. And get ready for bed. It's late, and it's a school night."

Lincoln looks out the window. The snowfall has

intensified. "I'm glad my dad is with my mom," he says.

"I'm glad, too. And I'm glad you're here with me, Link."

"Yeah. Thanks." He picks up the puppy, who has fallen asleep under the table, and lets her out, then he gently settles her into her crate. After dinner, Lucille makes the puppy a dog bed using an extra pillow and one of her flannel pillowcases. They both watch the dog settle in on it and close her eyes. "She loves it!" Lincoln says, and Lucille says, "Who wouldn't?"

Lincoln is in bed and almost asleep when Lucille comes in to say good night. He has moved the puppy's crate to be beside him, and the dog opens one eye to regard Lucille, then returns to sleep.

"I bet there won't be school tomorrow," Lincoln says.

"I know," Lucille says. "Those school administrators are a bunch of wusses. Wouldn't hurt you kids one bit to go to school when there's a little snow on the ground."

"They said on the TV that it could be a foot!"

"Oh, pooh, that's nothing. I used to walk to school in **three** feet of snow!"

Lincoln smiles. "That's such a stereotype."

As ever, Lucille is impressed at Lincoln's vocabulary. In some ways, kids today seem so much smarter. But they can't add in their heads anymore. They have no idea how to use the reference room in the library. They rely on their phones for everything, even socializing. Why don't they get off their phones and play Capture the Flag? At least Link loves to read. There's always hope when a kid—or an adult, for that matter—likes to read.

"What's a stereotype?" she asks him.

"The way old people always say how tough it was for them. And how we have it so easy now."

"You do!" Lucille says.

He shrugs. "Yeah, I guess. In some ways." He turns onto his side, away from her. "Good night, Lucille."

She feels bad about what she said. Worrying about your mother dying is hardly having it easy.

She pats his shoulder. "Call me if you need me, okay?"

"Okay."

"If there's no school tomorrow, know what we're going to do?"

"What?"

"Have a John Wayne movie marathon, that's what."

"Great," Lincoln says, and turns to look over his shoulder at her. "Really. I mean it. I like those movies."

"You mostly laugh at them."

"But I like them." He settles back onto his side. She smells him, little-boy smell mixed with soap—he loves her Lifebuoy soap.

Lucille sits on the edge of his bed. She looks out the window over the bed for a while, watching the snow fall. Then she says softly, in case Lincoln has fallen asleep already, "I used to be in love with John Wayne."

Link turns over, eyes wide. "Really?"

"Yes. I loved Gene Autry the best, but I loved John Wayne, too."

"Did you ever meet them?"

Lucille laughs. "Oh, good heavens, no. And if I did I probably would have fainted dead away."

"You probably wouldn't have liked them that much in person, anyway. You probably wouldn't have loved them, anyway."

"You think not?"

"No. Real love isn't like that. My dad says real love is when the other person is your best friend and you shouldn't have to work hard around them, it should be, like, more natural, and you just want to be with them even if you're not doing anything."

"You're right. And I did have a love like that. His name was Frank Pearson—isn't that a lovely name? Frank Pearson, but I only got to be with him for a little while. I loved him way back in high school but then he married someone else and he didn't even want to."

"Why did he marry her, then?"

"Well, that's not . . ."

"Was she pregnant?"

Lucille's mouth falls open.

Lincoln smiles.

"As a matter of fact, she **was** pregnant, and in those days, you did the honorable thing, and he married her. Then after many, many years she died, and he wrote me a letter when I was eighty-three. Eighty-three years old but I had never forgotten him, and I thought, what the heck. Well, we got together and we really liked each other and we were going to get married and then **he** died. He had a heart attack. I thought I'd die myself I hurt so bad after that, but I didn't. I'm still here."

He's looking at her in a whole new way. "So, you guys . . . like . . . dated?"

Lucille stands. "Okay. Good night, now."

She goes into her room and climbs into bed, turns off her bedside lamp. She stares into the darkness. That there is a child sleeping in her house, under her care. Huh. Things can certainly happen in a funny order.

When Lucille was a girl, a carnival came to town one summer and they had a ride called the Whirligig. You sat in some wooden contraption that jerked you here, there, and everywhere. One minute you'd be going forward, the next backward or sideways or tilted over so far you thought you might fall out. It was never still and you had no idea what might come next. That's life. You're born, and you get a ride on the Whirligig.

She yawns and feels herself falling into a deep sleep.


SOME WARMTH COMES TO her. It comes to her and in her and all around her. Kind of like a hot flash, only pleasant.

She opens her eyes to see a familiar figure at the side of her bed, his hands clasped in front of him like a shy person. She rolls her eyes. The angel is wearing jeans, a plaid flannel shirt, sneakers. His wings are awfully ratty for someone in service to the On High.

He extends a glowing hand. "Lucille Rachel Howard—"

"Not on your life," she says. "I'm babysitting a little boy tonight."

The angel looks confused.

"If you knew what you were doing, you would know perfectly well that I have a child sleeping right down the hall and I am not going to die and have him wake up alone with a corpse. That family needs me right now. Also, when it is time, I want Frank Pearson to escort me out of here, not you."

"I'm sorry, but I can't be influenced by anything. I have a job I must do."

Lucille wants to scream. She wants to at least yell. And so she gets out of bed and puts on her robe and gestures for the angel to follow her. She goes past Lincoln's room and looks in. All is quiet. With infinite care, she closes the door, then clomps downstairs, the angel kind of floating behind her.

She sits at the kitchen table and gestures to the other chair. The angel turns it sideways so that his wings can be accommodated. Then he sits down and folds his hands on the table. "You're making this awfully difficult for me," he tells Lucille.

"**I'm** making it difficult for **you**?"

"If you had come with me the first time, we wouldn't be in this pickle."

"If I had come with you the first time, Link wouldn't have had anyone to take care of him, and as you must know, he needs someone to take care of him because his mother is very sick and in the hospital. She's very sick; in fact, she . . ." Her face changes, and she leans in closer. "Say. You must know. Is she going to die? Or will she live?"

Nothing.

"For Pete's sake, tell me!"

His face assumes a look of great dignity. "It all depends."

"Well, of course it all depends!" Lucille says. "But can't you tell me what will happen? Or . . . can't you ask for a little favor? You must have some good connections!"

Nothing. She can see through him, just a bit. There on the shelf behind him are her favorite cookbooks, all lined up, and she can see **Hoosier Mama Book of Pies** and **Rosie's All-Butter Fresh Cream Sugar-Packed Baking Book.**

"Can you eat?" Lucille asks suddenly.

"No. Not really."

"What do you mean, not really?"

"Well, it's not necessary."

"But **can** you?"

"Honestly? I haven't tried."

Lucille lifts the foil off the platter of pinwheels that she and Lincoln made and pushes it toward him. "Try."

The angel regards the cookies, then lifts one up, puts it in his mouth, and chews. Then his expression changes, and fat tears roll down his face.

"What?" Lucille says, alarmed. "What's the matter?"

"I can taste him."

"Who?"

"The little boy. I can taste what he feels." He sits still for a moment. "All right, Miss Howard. You can stay." He stands and bumps into the table, then the chair. He shrugs and grins at Lucille—a crooked grin—then disappears. And Lucille gasps. **That smile!**

IN THE MORNING, LUCILLE has no time to spend thinking about yet another weird dream. She turns on the radio and hears that the schools are indeed closed. Also, the library's class on Polish paper cutting as well as tonight's performance of the Wham Bam Theater Company's production of **Pippin**. The AA meeting at the First Baptist will be moved to tomorrow, and the Knitters Club will reconvene at its usual time next week. "For heaven's sake," Lucille mutters, as she makes coffee. "It isn't the Apocalypse!"

After Lincoln awakens and lets both dogs out, Lucille makes the boy a toad in a hole and she says it's okay for him to share some toast with the animals.

At one point, Lincoln looks at her closely, then says, "Are you okay?"

"What do you mean?" she asks, dunking her toast in her coffee.

"I don't know. Don't get mad, but you look sick."

"I didn't sleep well, that's all. You see if, when you get old, **you** don't look like a cotton sheet left too long in the dryer when you don't sleep well."

He finishes his orange juice and brings his dishes to the sink.

"Why didn't you sleep well?" he asks.

What to say? "Oh, I've been having a nightmare that keeps recurring. Do you know what 'recurring' means?"

"Sure, it means coming back again and again."

She regards the boy with a mix of admiration and annoyance. "Tell me something. Can you spell 'eleemosynary'?"

"What's that?"

"It's a word. You don't know what it means, huh?"

"No. What's it mean?"

"It means of or pertaining to charity. Now try to spell it."

He sits down at the table and stares into her face, as though her expression will help him. Well, it won't. Lucille has a good poker face, it's just that she forgets to use it. But now she is totally impassive. A sphinx.

"E-L-I—"

"Nope. Ding-dong, you're wrong."

"Okay."

"Want to try again?"

"E-L-E-M—"

"Nope."

"E-L-A?"

"Three times and you're out!"

"So how do you spell it?" Lincoln asks, and when she tells him, he says "Really?"

"Really. You can look it up."

"No, I trust you. Cool, I learned a new word and I can fool my friends with how to spell it."

If there's one thing that Lucille hates, it's trying to badger somebody impervious to badgering.

Oh, but what is wrong with her? He's such a sweet kid. He can't help it if he's precocious. It's not like he brags about it. He can't hurt anyone by being smart. Lucille is just one big crab, on account of lack of sleep. She feels as irritable as can be.

Lincoln is staring at her.

"What?" she asks.

"What was your nightmare about?"

"I don't remember, really."

Lincoln nods sympathetically. "Yeah, sometimes even when you can't remember, it still scares you."

"Right."

"When I was little, like three or four? I used to dream every night about Jelly Man. Every night, I swear. He was just a man made of jelly but to me he was really, really scary. He had these big black holes for eyes, and he would come into my room and just stand there."

"Well, that's enough, isn't it, to have someone come in your room and just stand by your bed. It's just . . . It's just invasive."

"Yeah." Lincoln picks up the puppy and puts her in his lap. "I thought of a name for my dog. And guess what, it was in a dream I had last night."

"Really?"

"Yeah, a man was standing at my bed, like Jelly Man, only he was nice. And he was not jelly, he was just a man. And he leaned over and whispered in my ear, 'Hope.' So that's the puppy's name!"

"Well, that's a very nice name. But the man . . . do you know what he looked like?"

"No, I didn't see him very well. I didn't see his face. All I remember is that he was wearing jeans and a flannel shirt."

Lucille's mouth goes dry. "Is that so."

"Yup." He sets his puppy on the floor. "Want to go out, Hope?"

The tail, round and round.

"Okay. Come!"

The puppy follows him to the back door, he opens it to let her out, then comes in to put on his coat and boots. "There's a lot of snow! Can we stay out for a while?"

"Of course."

Lucille sits still, staring into her empty coffee cup. So what. He didn't say the man in his dream was wearing a plaid shirt, and he said nothing about seeing any wings. Maybe she and Lincoln just shared the same kind of dream because they were sleeping under the same roof. It could happen.

She is about to wash up the dishes when the phone

rings. Iris, no doubt, asking when she should come today.

But it's not Iris. It's Jason, asking to speak to his son, and his voice is rigid-sounding, almost mean. At first, Lucille thinks, **Wait, is he angry at me for teasing Lincoln?** But he doesn't know about that. And then he says, "Oh, Lucille . . ." and a big sword of ice plunges straight down the center of Lucille's spine. He says Abby's alive, but she's way worse. Jason needs to get Link out to the hospital, but he can't leave his wife.

Lucille closes her eyes. It's one thing to lose the love of your life at eighty-three. It's another to lose your mother when you're just a little boy.

But Lucille knows what to do. "I'll call Tiny Dawson," she tells Jason. "He's my friend and he's a very nice man and he has a truck and I know he'll be glad to drive Link there."

"Oh, thank God. I'll pay him."

"That's what you think. You just try to pay Tiny for a favor."

# An Invitation

———

Tiny is in his truck, ready to go and pick up Lincoln, when his phone rings again. Lucille, he bets. "Almost there," he says, answering. "Took a while to dig myself out."

Silence, and he realizes it might be a customer. "Best Taxi," he says.

"Tiny?"

Monica! His heart moves into his throat and he is temporarily speechless.

"Tiny?" she says again.

"Hey, Monica. How are you?"

"Well, I can't move an inch out there! Have you been out?"

"I am out."

"So you're working today?"

"Not really. Not yet. Got to do something else first."

"Well, could you . . . I'm sorry to ask, Tiny, I truly am, but I need to get to work. Polly's in California, you know, and I'm the only one with keys to open up. And I cannot get my car out, the snow's too deep and I think it's iced in, besides. I can't think of any-one else who might help. In return, I'll give you breakfast on the house, whatever you want."

"I'll come and get you. But I can't stay for break-fast, I have to give someone else a ride somewhere. What's your address?"

"One forty-seven Laurel."

"One forty-seven Laurel? I been past your place a million times, and never even knew you lived there."

"Well, I do. I do, and, Tiny, I . . ."

He waits, but she only adds, "I'll be right at the window, looking out for you."

When he reaches her house, he sees her on the porch, a pretty woman dressed in a red coat. He looks in the rearview, wets his hand, and smooths down his hair.

Monica climbs into his truck and snaps the safety belt. "Whew!" she says. "I can't tell you how grateful I am. I know people will be out and about soon, wanting their breakfasts. Sometimes on the worst weather days is when we have our best business." She hands him a paper bag. "I put a little something in here. It's just a muffin and an orange. And it's a healthy muffin. I'm trying to lose a few pounds."

"You don't need to lose anything!" Tiny says. "You're absolutely perfect the way you are!"

Well, now he's done it. Dan used to tell him, "If

you want to chase a woman away, just heap praise on her. I'm telling you, they like the mean ones." Tiny isn't so sure about that. And anyway, it's not his nature to treat anyone unkindly. Even in high school, he was known as a big softie who could drop you in one punch if he wanted to. But he never wanted to.

When Tiny pulls into the parking lot, there are already two cars waiting.

"See?" Monica says.

"'Least your lot got plowed," Tiny says.

"Yeah, he's good. Jack Bessel. You know him?"

"I know him," Tiny says. Old guy. No competition.

"Thanks again," Monica says. She puts her hand to the door handle, then turns to look at him. "Would you like to come back for a free lunch?"

"Can't, sorry," Tiny says. He won't be back by then.

Monica is embarrassed, he can see it. Now she's the one who's been rejected. And he feels bad, so he says, "How about . . ." He clears his throat. "How about if we have dinner tonight?"

He's barely got the words out before she says yes. "Come over around seven," she says. "I'll make you dinner."

He watches her wave at a customer getting out of his car, watches her pull out the keys and open the restaurant. She turns back and waves at him with a kind of solemnity he can't figure out. What a mysterious sex.

He heads over to Lucille Howard's house. She

wants him to take this kid to Columbia. It will take a bit longer than usual, but he'll do it. Of course he will. Kid's mother is dying. What a thing. He wonders what he can talk about to take the kid's mind off it. Nothing, that's what.

# A Truck Ride

HALFWAY TO COLUMBIA, THE SNOW HAS ALL but disappeared. Only a few flakes fly around wildly, seeming to want to make up in ferocity what is lacking in number. The ride thus far has been mostly silent. Now Tiny asks Lincoln, "You like sports?"

"Not really."

"Not even baseball?"

"It's okay, I guess."

The kid is worrying a little hole in the knee of his jeans.

"You keep picking at that thing, you're going to feel a draft."

Lincoln folds his hands in his lap.

"I'm just fooling with you," Tiny says, and the kid says nothing.

"You hungry?" he asks. "I got a muffin in here."

"No, I'm good."

Tiny looks over at him. Cute kid. "You worried?" he asks. Might as well see if he wants to talk about it.

Lincoln looks back at him. "No."

Okay, then.

After a while, Tiny says, "Hey, Lincoln. You know how to drive a stick shift?"

"I don't drive."

"That ain't what I asked you."

"No, I don't know how to drive a stick shift."

"Want me to teach you? We got another little while before we get there. If you want, I'll teach you how to shift before we get there."

"Okay." The kid tightens his mouth, holding back a grin, Tiny thinks.

Well, now he's done it. But next time they come to a stoplight, he'll have the kid put the truck into first, then second. He'll talk to him about clutches, about timing, about feeling things out so you know when it's time to switch gears. Then, after the kid has shifted a few times, he'll say, "Look at that, you're a natural. I'll have to get an application over to you right away so you can come and work for me."

# Waiting

I N THE HALL OUTSIDE ABBY'S ROOM, JASON IS
talking to her doctor.

"So it's pretty much over?" he asks.

"It's hard to say."

"Right."

"It really is hard to say. I know that sounds like
nothing, but it's actually hopeful."

"She can't even lift her hand."

"I know. She's in tough shape, and it's possible . . .
I'm glad you called your son."

Jason offers a bitter laugh.

"It might still work."

Jason nods, and the doctor walks away to join his
team, who have kept a respectful and sorrowful
distance.

At the end of the hall, Jason sees Lincoln with

a tall, overweight man. He walks over to meet them.

"Tiny?"

Tiny offers his hand. "Yes, sir. Brought you your son. And it was a pleasure."

"I'm so grateful. Thank you so much. I'd be very glad if I could pay you."

Tiny backs away, one hand held up. "Ain't no need. We had a good time. Your son is now a champion shifter."

"A what?"

"I taught him how to shift my truck."

"He **drove**?"

"Nah, he just shifted a few times. But he's got it."

"Dad?"

"Yeah?"

"Can I go in and see her?"

"Let's go together." Jason nods goodbye to Tiny and starts down the hall. "I don't want you to be alarmed, son. She looks a little wiped out."

"I know."

"How do you know?"

Lincoln shrugs.

When they push the door open to Abby's room, she appears to be asleep, but Jason looks quickly to make sure her chest is rising and falling. She's got a nasal cannula on to deliver oxygen and an IV set for a slow drip. Jason meant to tell Lincoln about the cannula, but it doesn't seem to bother him.

He stands looking at his mother and Jason points to the cannula. "That's giving her oxygen so that she can breathe a little better, that's all that is."

Lincoln looks up at him, tears in his eyes. "She can't breathe?"

"No, no, she can breathe. This just helps."

Lincoln sits on the chair and removes his shoes. Then he climbs in bed beside his mother, who does not respond.

Jason hopes no one comes in and tells Lincoln to get off the bed. Because he would have to kill that person.

He sits in the chair and watches as Lincoln touches his mother's hand, then holds it.

"The puppy has a name," he tells her.

Nothing.

Lincoln moves closer to Abby and closes his eyes. Jason watches them. Rubs his hands together. Watches.

# One Last Try

═══

IRIS RIPS UP THE CARD WITH THE BEAUTIFUL photo of the cardinal. She wrote to Ed again. She said things that didn't quite express what she wanted, as usual. She looks at her watch. Half an hour before she has to leave to go to Lucille's. Outside, she can hear the plows, and the sun is beginning to melt the snow that lies on her windowsill. She has time.

She picks out another card, which shows a boulder in a field, and on it a single word is carved: KIND-NESS. She starts to write on the card, then doesn't. She'll only rip it up, and that would be a shame.

Her computer pings with a message, but it's only an ad. She deletes it, then sits before her screen, thinking. She still knows his email address, unless he has changed it.

She types his address in the bar, and on the subject line, puts: **Please read.**

Down to the body of the email.

Just do it.

Do it.

She goes to the kitchen for a glass of water, then approaches the desk chair as though sneaking up on it. She sits down. Thinks. Then she stops thinking and just begins typing.

**Dear Ed,**

**I have written notes to you so many times, but I never mail them. I suppose I understand that you're not exactly eager to hear from me, and I don't blame you for that. But I hope you'll bear with me while I try to explain some things to you. To unburden my heart, if you'll excuse a little New Age talk one last time.**

**In the days after I asked you for a divorce, I had to move away from any feelings for you, because I felt bound to do what I said I would do. I could only look in one direction. That day in court, I remember I showed you a new purse I'd gotten, as though we were still together. And you looked at it and said, "That's really nice," and I got a rush of feeling that made me think I was going to burst into tears and so I looked away from you and never looked at you again, even after it was all over and we were leaving the room, and then the building, together. I watched you walk to your car with your back so straight. I must**

have seemed so heartless to you, but I was overwhelmed with sorrow that I had hurt you so. The few times I saw you after that, with Kathleen, it seemed like you were racing along and I was glued to the earth. And that last time I saw you, and I saw that Kathleen was pregnant, well, that was what made me move from Boston. Which you might not even know. But I left Boston to live in a small town in Missouri. Mason, it's called. You might remember that I always did kind of want to live in a small town.

I want to say that it was not your fault, our divorce, it was both of ours. I am so very sorry for the pain you endured and I never got the chance to tell you that, and I guess I am writing now to ask your forgiveness. It would mean an awful lot to me if you could just tell me you forgive me.

Iris's throat begins to hurt, two parallel lines on either side.

Finish.

There was a selfishness in me when I was married to you and I still am not sure why. I could blame it on my youth, I suppose, but everything about that notion rings false. Rather, I think that it was that I was afraid of wanting something so much.

You met my family, and you heard a lot of

stories of my growing up. You know that it was a lonely place for me to be, when I lived at home. I had no allies in my siblings, we all lived in our own separate orbits. Every night, the four of us shut in our rooms, after having had a silent dinner with parents who were miserable with each other. I wanted something so bad. I was dying for something.

And then I met you. And you were . . . Well, even, is what you were. Even and kind, and you'd go along with things, like the time we were driving somewhere and I told you I was surprised I'd never smoked, I always thought I might like to smoke and that I would have been a good smoker, whatever that meant, but you went into a store and got us a pack of Marlboros and we sat in the car and you lit two cigarettes like that guy in the old movie and then we tried to smoke but we began to cough and then to laugh and then we just threw the pack away.

There are so many memories that are precious to me. You brought me a bird's nest once, and whispered over it as though it were sacred, which, to me, it was. In our last years together, you made me dinner every Sunday night and I never told you how I relished the sounds of your cooking while I lay on the sofa and read. And I know I complimented you on the food, but I don't think I ever

thanked you for the regularity of your cooking, the way I could count on it.

Oh, and that you could fix everything.
That you would cover me with a blanket
when I fell asleep on the couch. That you told
me how an airplane flies, in great detail, over
and over until I really got it. That you knew
every member of the cabinet, that you
knew your geography. That I don't think I
ever heard you yell, except the night after
I told you I wanted out and then you yelled
and wept and I remember I thought in that
moment that someone should strike me
down for making someone so otherwise gentle do that.

It occurs to me that right about now you
might be feeling creepy, thinking I'm trying
to come back into your life. Please believe me
when I tell you that I have never stopped
loving you and doubt I ever will, but what I
am trying to do is not get into your life, but
to get you out of mine. In the nicest of ways.

It would mean so much to me if you would
write back to say that you forgive me. If
appearances mean anything, I know that
you're happy, that you've moved on, and I
doubt that I ever cross your mind.

But I guess I'm asking you to see me
in your mind's eye and offer a simple yes.
If you'd just send me back a message saying,

Yes. Or maybe you could go all out and say, Yes, I forgive you.

I'm not going to effectively rip this email up and delete it. I'm not going to re-read it, either. I'm just going to send it and hope—

Well, you know what I really hope? I hope you are rich in love, now and forever. . . .

                                                          Iris

She pushes Send. Then she goes into the Sent file and deletes her message.

What will be, will be.

She stands, and her legs seem weak to her. Then they are not, and she gathers up her things to go over to Lucille's. She loves that old lady. She loves their business. Feeding people, making people happy.

# Quitsville

———

PHIL IS BACK IN TOWN AFTER A QUICK TRIP, and he's on the way to Monica's, expecting to spend the night with her. But Monica has something else in mind.

"Phil," she says, after letting him in the door. "Before you sit down, I want to tell you something."

"Aw, Christ," he says. "Is this about the ring? I told you I'd get it. Give a guy some time."

"No, it's not about the ring."

He smiles his killer smile. "Good. Good girl."

"Or maybe it is."

His smile fades and she can see he is about to offer some other lame excuse.

"I don't want the ring," she says.

"Oh, yes you do."

The nerve!

"Phil, you know, I thought you were someone

else. I thought you might be the one for me, but nothing could be further from the truth. And so I'm sorry, but I don't want to see you anymore. I don't want you coming here and I'd appreciate it if you didn't come into my restaurant anymore, either."

"I can go into that restaurant whenever I want."

"We'll see about that."

"Monica, what have you got stuck up your butt?"

"Ew," she says, quietly. And then, "Look, don't let's waste any more time on this. On us. We're done."

"**Why?**"

"Because I say so."

He stands looking at her. Then he says, "I never intended to get you a ring."

"I knew that."

"No you didn't."

"Goodbye, Phil."

He starts to say something, thinks better of it, and then he is gone.

Monica leans against the door, her heart pounding. For one moment, almost as an autonomic response, she starts to feel bad. But then the voice of her mother comes into her head, saying, "I'm right proud of you, honey."

# Who's the Boss?

—

"WELL, YOU'RE JUST DOING EVERYTHING," Lucille says.

Iris looks over at her from the refrigerator, where she is putting away the groceries she shopped for before she came over.

"I want to," Iris says. "I like learning all this."

"You've learned a lot, and fast."

"Thanks!"

Lucille looks like hell, and she huffs and puffs whenever she walks. Iris was so alarmed when she first arrived, she tried to get Lucille to go to bed. **That** went well:

Iris, coming in the door: Oh, my goodness. Are you okay?

Lucille: What are you talking about?

Iris: Well, you look . . . Are you okay?

Lucille: Of course I'm okay, we have things to do.

Iris: I know, but maybe you should lie down a little bit first.

Lucille: Why?

Iris: I mean . . . you look tired.

Lucille: And you look anxious. And like a busy-body. Maybe **you** want to lie down.

Iris: Okay, Lucille.

Lucille: If I wanted to lie down, I would lie down.

It has begun to occur to Iris that Lucille is a friend, Lucille and Tiny and Monica are all friends. Astonishing—and humiliating!—to see that she didn't have friends in Boston. All those years, and not one person that she had truly opened up to, or kept up with. Probably she expected her husband to be everything to her when it wasn't his place to do that, even if he wanted to or could. Another thing she regrets: having made him feel that he was failing her when she was the one failing herself.

She feels as though she has become a truer version of herself. She never used to believe that where you lived mattered that much. But maybe it does.

Lucille asks, "Did you say you got the butter? The Plugrá?"

"Yes. I got everything on the list. But before we get going, can I make you some soup? We have time."

"Soup!"

"Yes. Tomato soup. All I need is an onion and some butter and a can of crushed tomatoes. It cooks up really fast and it's just delicious."

Lucille scowled. "Who said anything about soup?

We're going to make snowflake cookies and lace angel cookies. Now, what shall we do first?"

"You should sit down. I should start some soup. While it's cooking, I want to see if I can assemble everything we need without your telling me. I would love to learn that. Will you let me do that—try to set things up—and then tell me what I missed?"

"Oh, for cripe's sake. All right. But just let me empty the dish drainer, let me dry those few things."

"I'll do it. And you know, you could lie down until—"

"If you say that again, I might go after you with the rolling pin."

Silence, as Iris peruses Lucille's pantry, then takes down a can of crushed tomatoes. "You've got avocado, right? I could make tortilla soup, too."

"Too spicy," says Lucille. "Give me some good corn chowder over a spicy soup any day."

"You want that? I'll make—"

"Not now! Did you get the cake flour and superfine sugar?"

"Yup."

"Double-strength vanilla?"

"I got everything, I told you."

Lucille takes in a deep breath and looks out the window.

"You okay?" Iris asks.

"Stop **asking** me that! We have a lot to do. And there's two **men** in the class today."

"Great!"

"I know," says Lucille. "Maybe we should do tuxedo cookies, too." She holds on to the edge of the table to take in another deep breath and Iris says not one word. When she serves the soup, Lucille does not eat, but rather loads it up on the spoon and then dumps it back into the bowl in a way that she must think Iris doesn't see. But she does.


As they are cleaning up after class, Lucille says, "Maybe I'll start teaching fewer classes and make more cakes for the restaurant."

Iris speaks carefully. "Oh?"

"Can't do both anymore."

"The money would be about the same either way."

"I don't care about the money," Lucille says. "I just want to reach people."

"Ah," Iris says.

"I thought I wanted to teach, but I don't think most of my students go home and do what I tell them. They just come to socialize. It's a different world. People don't bake from scratch anymore."

"Sure they do!"

"Not like they should. Not like they could. No, they want to look at those housewives on television and eat ready-made desserts."

"Well, I've begun to bake from scratch because of you," Iris says.

"Oh? What do you bake? What did you last make and when did you make it?"

Iris looks her right in the eye and tells her. "Two

days ago, I made midnight cake and I ate two pieces and then I froze the rest to eat later. Tomorrow, I'm making butterscotch dreams. And I'm bringing most of them to the nursing home. Last week I brought them four dozen of your cream-cheese–lemon bars and they lasted about two seconds."

"Really?" Lucille asks, her dishtowel pressed against her bosom.

"There was practically a riot. And I always bring the cookies over in one of our boxes, and last week one of the residents found it so pretty she asked if she could have it to keep her curlers in. Naturally, I said yes."

"Huh," Lucille says. "But you really ought to bring them the prune-whip bars."

"I'll do it next week," Iris says.

# It's Only Words

W HEN SHE GETS HOME, IRIS STOPS BY
Tiny's apartment to deliver some soup. She'd
wanted to bring him cookies, but she knows not to.
She knocks, but there's no answer. Not home yet.

She goes into her own apartment and greets
Homer, then picks him up, turns him belly side up,
and scratches him. "Did you miss me?"

The cat closes his eyes.

"You did, didn't you?"

She keeps the cat in her arms as she goes around
turning lights on. They worked late tonight, she
and Lucille, no matter Iris's concerns for her. Lucille
said she'd be a hundred percent better in the morning.

Iris opens her refrigerator and inspects the contents.
Leftover turkey meatloaf and mashed potatoes. That

sounds good, and she'll sauté a little spinach with garlic.

She puts the meatloaf and potatoes in the oven and then goes to check her email.

When the screen comes up, she gasps. Ed Winters.

She gets up and walks around the room, her arms tightly crossed. And then she sits before her computer and opens the email:

> Iris,
>
> Quite a surprise to hear from you. I'm glad you wrote, because I have something to say to you.
>
> It may be true that you owe me an apology—you were pretty harsh. But maybe I deserved it.
>
> Iris, I really hope it doesn't hurt you for me to say this, but I dismissed your longing for a baby as cruelly as you ever treated me. The truth is, I need your forgiveness as much as you need mine. Every time I look at my child, I know I was wrong.
>
> So how about this. Let's forgive each other. And then we'll have said the proper and loving goodbye to which we both were entitled.
>
> > Be well, Iris.
> >
> > Ed

Iris goes into the kitchen, where the timer is going off. She shuts it off, takes out the meatloaf and the potatoes, spills some oil in a pan to heat up so that she can prepare the spinach. Then she turns off the flame and goes to her bed and lies down and grabs a pillow and sobs. She'll cry for a long time, she can tell. But after she's done crying, she'll have such a good dinner.

# A Declaration

———

AT SEVEN O'CLOCK, TINY IS STANDING ON Monica's doorstep. It's a few days after she cooked for him, and now he's taking her to a restaurant Iris told him about where there are candles on the tables. He got his hair cut. He's wearing a new pair of khaki-colored pants he got at Costco and they are a bit tight in the waist but they fit. He ironed a white shirt, which required no small effort. He put on a small amount of aftershave. Now he rings the doorbell and when she opens the door, she smiles. She's wearing a pink dress and Lord have mercy.

He draws himself up. "Monica? I am tired of messing around. I love you, and that's all there is to it. I have for a long time."

Monica's eyes fill with tears. "I love you, too, you big dope. I only was with someone else because

I thought you didn't care for me. Well, that and I thought he was my destiny."

"Really?"

She laughs. "I went to see a fortune-teller when Polly and I went to New Orleans, and she said I would marry a man whose name started with a **P.** And so when I met Phil Porter, I thought, **Well, this is it!**"

Tiny says nothing, and she says, "I know. I know that's so dumb."

"Monica?"

"Yes?"

"Can I tell you something?"

"Of course!"

"But you can never tell anyone else. This will be our first thing that is only between you and me. One of those couple things. A secret that only the two of us share."

"What is it?"

"Well, first you have to promise me you'll never tell."

"I promise, I sincerely do."

"You want to know my name?"

She frowns. "I know your name!"

"Tiny is a nickname. My real name . . . Okay, my real name is Percival." He feels a deep heat rise up in his face.

"Ohhhh," Monica says softly. She stands there looking up at him.

He starts to speak but she interrupts him. "Okay, first of all? I love that name." When he starts to protest, she says, "I do! I used to play princess with my best friend Terry Thompson and she would be Princess Lucivia and I would be Princess Eleanora. And we had prince boyfriends. Hers was Prince Charles, which I thought was awfully unoriginal. But mine? Mine was Prince Percival."

"You're kidding. Are you kidding?"

"I swear it's true. I might even have proof. We used to make these drawings, and I put Prince Percival in a purple mantle with ermine trim and I wrote his name all around his head like an aura. Prince Percival! I really might have proof. My mom saved almost all my drawings and I have them in a big steamer trunk. I could find them. I'm pretty sure I could."

"Monica?"

"Yes?"

"I believe you."

"Well, okay then."

They stand there grinning at each other, and then Monica shivers and says, "Well, for Pete's sake, come in while I get my coat, and then let's get going."

# Negotiations

———

LUCILLE CANNOT GET OUT OF THE BATHTUB. SHE has tried and tried, and she cannot get out. What to do. She leans back in the cooling water and closes her eyes.

"Lucille Rachel Howard," she hears.

She gasps and sits up, tries to cover herself with her washcloth. It doesn't go far.

"What is the matter with you?" she says. "I am bare naked."

"You are as you were when you came into this world."

"Well, I am not going out this way, I can tell you that."

"It's time, Lucille."

"But I'm naked!"

"Even so."

"I just want to make Maddy's wedding cake. Can't

I just do that one thing, make Maddy's cake? Chocolate and vanilla checkerboard, she'll be so surprised."

"I'm sorry, no."

"You're killing me!"

A one-shouldered shrug. "Effectively, I suppose."

"Please," she says. "Please just let me do one more thing, all I'm asking for is to do one more thing."

"Yes," the angel says, "everyone asks for one more thing. But I'm afraid we're out of time." His voice is not without compassion.

"But what about my miracle? I wanted a miracle and you said I could have one."

"I didn't say that. But in fact, you can. You can have a miracle before you go."

Oh, what relief washes over her. "Okay. Good. So what I want is for Lincoln's mother to live. Okay? That's what I want, let Abby live. And now I'm ready for Frank." She closes her eyes. So this will be the last thing she ever saw: Tub water. A bar of Lifebuoy. A pink washrag, and an angel.

"That would be two miracles, Lucille."

She opens her eyes. "What? What do you mean?"

"It would be two miracles, if Frank came for you and if Abby lived. You have to choose."

"But I . . ."

"Choose one, Lucille. Look into your heart for the answer."

Lucille draws in a huge breath, clasps her hands together, and squeezes her eyes shut. She will choose Abby, she will, she will; let her last act be an unselfish one. But then she begins to wail, and she says, "I looked into my heart, and what my heart wants is Frank!"

"Then you must choose him. And now, **finally:** Lucille Rachel Howard, I am the angel of death and I have come to take you home."

"But can I just ask, what did **you** want, before you died?" Maybe he was selfish, too, and he still got into heaven.

The angel smiles. "What did I want?" He looks around her bathroom as though it is the Louvre.

"Oh," Lucille says. "I see." She hears a door opening. She hears water running. The song of a finch. She tastes vanilla. Bread and butter. She feels a breeze. She sees swiftly moving cirrus clouds against deep blue, a kind of ocean in the sky, she hears the beckoning voice of her one true love, and now he is here before her. Frank Pearson.

Something in Lucille's chest bears down hard, harder, oh, it's astonishing, she didn't know anything could be this painful. And then it stops. It stops, and a deep silence descends.

She rises up as easily as she did as a girl, and she reaches for Frank's hand.

She is wearing a necklace of stars.

# Hungry

———

Jason has fallen asleep in his chair next to Abby's bed when he is awakened by Lincoln, tapping his arm. He squints at his watch: 11:50 P.M.

They set up a cot for Link in the corner of the room and piled on blankets and pillows. "Cool, a nest," he said, trying to be enthusiastic about something in this strange place. But he hasn't slept; nothing on the cot has been disturbed.

Jason quickly checks Abby. Nothing different, she's lying on her back, her mouth slighty open, and she's breathing quietly, none of the gurgling sounds that she makes when she needs to be suctioned. It's terrible when they do that, Jason won't let Link be in the room when they do that. He's relieved to leave the room himself when they do that. **The notions we have!** he has often thought, being here. The way we seem to believe our deaths will be simple and neat: like falling asleep. Here, then gone. **Poof!** None of the indignities that have been visited upon Abby, and she's not even the worst case.

He puts an arm around Lincoln. "What's up, buddy?"

"Can we go and get something to eat?"

Jason isn't sure what to do. He doesn't want to send Link off alone, and he doesn't want to leave his wife's side. He's heard often enough that people wait to be alone to die. He doesn't want her to die. She can't die.

"Please, Dad? Just quickly? I'm so hungry. We can just get something from the vending machine."

Jason stands, offers his hand to Link.

They go out into the hall and Jason tells the night nurse behind the desk where they're headed. "We'll only be gone a minute; we'll be right back. I have my cell. You have my number."

The nurse—a sweet-looking woman named Laurie who told Jason and Lincoln that she'd been a nurse for thirty-five years—says, "Take your time. I'll sit with her."

"Can we get anything for you?" Jason asks.

"Aren't you sweet. No, I'm fine." She closes out of whatever she's doing on the computer, dons the sweater she has hanging on the back of her chair, and goes into Abby's room. One thing Jason is grateful for is how close Abby is to the nurses' station: he could practically whisper for help and be heard.

In the main lobby, Lincoln gets a Kind bar and a

cheese sandwich. On the way back to the elevator, they pass the gift shop, closed now, and Lincoln stops abruptly. He points to a stuffed animal in the window. "Dad! That looks exactly like Hope. Can we get it for Mom tomorrow?"

"Sure. If it's still there."

Lincoln looks quickly up at him. "Why wouldn't it be? It's not even open now, and I can come down as soon as . . ." He looks at the sign on the door. "I'll come down tomorrow morning at ten, right when they open."

"That'll be fine." He wants to slap himself for saying what he did. Not hard to figure out what's lurking in his mind.

In the elevator, Link opens the Kind bar and offers his father a bite.

"No thanks, Lincoln. You have it."

"You aren't hungry?"

Jason has no idea if he's hungry or not. But he shakes his head no.

"Dad? Did you know it was that nurse, Laurie, who gave Mom the lucky handkerchief?"

Jason smiles. "Yeah, I did know that. She asked if she could tape it there on the wall over Mom's head. I figured it couldn't hurt, right?"

"Right. It has four-leaf clovers on it."

"I saw."

"Laurie said when she brings it to the casino, she always wins."

"Well, there you go."

Jason feels a kind of irrational burst of anger: the **casino**! But you can't custom-order people's kindnesses. People do what they can, they give what they have. He has no right to be angry with someone who is just trying to help. He's not thinking the way he usually does: he has become someone unconsciously—or not so unconsciously—searching for something to be mad at, from cold coffee to the infuriating vagueness expressed every day by the medical community. **Hard to say. Can't be sure. Just have to wait and see.**

After they get to their floor, Jason tells Lincoln to go ahead, he'll be right there, he just wants to stop in the men's room. He doesn't like using Abby's bathroom, with all its weird medical equipment: something to clean out bedpans, something to measure urine, something to check for blood. A normal men's room seems like a luxury.

When he washes his hands, Jason sees himself in the mirror. He doesn't look much better than his wife does, really. He's got to get it together, for Lincoln and for Abby. In the morning, when the doctors make rounds, he'll press them to tell him what he should be thinking about, planning for. What should he tell his son? He can't keep telling Link they don't know, they don't know.

When he comes out of the bathroom, the nurse is back behind the desk on the phone, and Lincoln is standing with one foot in Abby's room, one foot in the hall. "Dad! Hurry up!"

He runs into the room. Abby is turned onto her side and is now facing them.

Her eyes are open, blinking, as though she is focusing, and then she smiles. "Jason."

Jason pulls Link to him and bends to speak into the boy's ear. "Can you go and get the nurse?"

"What time is it?" Abby asks.

Jason walks over to her and puts his hands on either side of her face. He touches his forehead to hers. The fever she had is gone; her skin is cool. Her eyes are bright. She's **here.**

"Are you okay?" Abby asks.

He laughs. "Yeah. I'm okay."

"Where's Lincoln?"

"Just out in the hall. He'll be right back."

"Have I been sleeping long?"

"Um . . . couple of days?"

"Oh, my goodness, you must have been so bored!"

"No, we weren't **bored.**"

"Were you scared?"

"Yes."

"I'm sorry."

He kisses her hand. "Don't be sorry."

"Jason, the strangest thing just happened. A woman was beside my bed, kind of a big woman. And she leaned down and embraced me and then I . . . I don't know, I woke up."

"Was it Laurie?"

"Who's that?"

"The nurse? She's really been pulling for you."

"No, it wasn't a nurse. I don't know who it was."

Abby's doctor comes in then and goes to her bed-side. "How are you feeling?"

"Hungry!" she says, and laughs.

"Looks like that treatment worked," he says. "You should feel even better in the morning. We're going to get you home, Abby."

# News

I RIS AWAKENS LATER THAN USUAL. SHE'S GOING
to be **tardy,** as Lucille will say. She tries calling to
let her know, but there is no answer. She's probably
in the bathroom; Iris will make coffee and call again.

No answer.

Something is wrong.

Iris dresses quickly, gets in the car, and drives over.
She parks way too far from the curb, and goes up to
the front door. Knocks, rings the bell. Does it again.
Nothing. She lets herself in, calls Lucille's name a
few times, and ventures upstairs.

She finds her in the bathtub, a pink washrag gripped
in her hand, her face a color that leaves little doubt
what has happened. Nonetheless Iris shouts "Lucille!,"
drops to her knees, and pulls the woman close to her.
She checks her wrist for a pulse, then presses in at the
side of her neck. No.

She holds Lucille close, weeping. After a while, she calls 911, then drains the tub, covers Lucille with a towel, and calls Tiny, to help her do whatever else needs to be done.

Tiny is asleep in Monica's bed, and he starts when his phone rings. His ringtone is "When a Man Loves a Woman," and he had put it on his phone thinking of Monica. And now there she is beside him, her long black hair spread out on the pillow like a Vargas girl. She stirs when she hears him whisper, "Best Taxi," and then, "Oh, no."

"What happened?" Monica asks, and Tiny holds up a finger.

"Are you there with her right now?"

He listens, wipes at his eyes, and says, "Don't worry, I'll take care of everything. I'm on the way."

He hangs up, and says, "That was Iris. Lucille Howard died. I've got to go over and help her. She found her in the bathtub."

"I'll come, too," Monica says. "I can . . . I'll make breakfast for everyone."

They drive together to Lucille's house, silent, holding hands. One life ends, another begins, is what Tiny is thinking, and by "another life" he is thinking of his and Monica's life together. He hopes it isn't wrong to feel that way, to want to keep happiness alive even while you admit sorrow. But when he looks over at Monica, he thinks maybe she is thinking that, too, so he feels a little better.

———

WHEN MADDY'S PHONE RINGS later that day, she's playing Candy Land with Nola after lunch, and she is very glad for the interruption; she hates Candy Land, though she does her best to disguise it. But then, after she hangs up, she comes into the kitchen and Nola says, "Mommy?" and Maddy bursts into tears.

She pulls her daughter onto her lap. "Nola, sweetheart? I have some sad news. Grandma Lucille died last night."

The little girl looks up into Maddy's face. "Is she in heaven?"

**Whatever heaven is,** Maddy thinks, but she tells her daughter, "I think so. Yes."

She holds Nola for a while, and then she calls Matthew. After that, she tells Nola, "We need to pack."

"I made a new drawing for her," Nola says, her eyes full of tears, and Maddy guesses the news is beginning to sink in.

"I think she'd want it on her wall," Maddy says. "We'll put it there."

# A Message

———

MADDY STANDS, SHIVERING, AT LUCILLE'S NEWLY dug gravesite. She knows she should leave, she's been standing here a good twenty minutes. Off to the side, two men in a small white truck wait patiently to lower the casket, then cover it with the mound of earth that now lies beneath a plastic tarp—like an elephant trying to hide behind a telephone pole, Maddy thinks. But something hasn't happened yet that she's waiting for, she's not even sure what. She gives the men a little wave, **I'm almost done,** and they wave back, **Take your time.**

In the car, Matthew and Nola are also waiting for her. Matthew is playing card games with Nola; he carries a kid-size deck for times when they must wait for things. Maddy is so grateful for the close relationship he's formed with Nola. When Nola is cold, Matthew enfolds her in his coat. When she's testy, he's the one who can best humor her out of it. When they go to movies, she sits on Matthew's lap. Any fears Maddy had that having a daughter would make it difficult to have a relationship with someone have long since faded: from the beginning, Matthew made it clear that for him, Nola was a bonus.

Iris has gone back to Lucille's house to prepare for anyone who might want to stop by. Maddy suspects there won't be many people who come; only a few people came to the church service: Maddy, Matthew, and Nola; Iris; Jason and Lincoln from next door; Tiny Dawson and Monica Mayhew.

Maddy had heard a lot about Iris from Lucille, and had looked forward to meeting her at the happy occasion of her and Matthew's wedding. Which now . . . Well, what? What should she do now? It doesn't make much sense for her to have the wedding here, now. No cake by Lucille. No attendance by Lucille. Or Arthur. How happy Arthur would have been for her!

She walks over a few rows to Arthur's grave— Arthur Moses, though she called him Truluv, her affectionate nickname for a man who never stopped loving his wife. Or the world. There he is, some part of him, anyway. More present is the memory of him that Maddy keeps alive in her heart. No one ever did more for her than Arthur Truluv did, and all because of an accidental meeting that happened here, in the oddest of places. And what happened here is what started her off in a new direction. Marrying Matthew and moving to New York is another direction, and she thinks Arthur would be thrilled for her. Lucille, too—eventually. Lucille was firmly fixed in her ideas about the city being a terrible place; Maddy was just as firmly fixed in her own ideas that a little time in the right places would change Lucille's mind. But. There are plans, and then there is life. She had planned to be married in Lucille's house this spring, to feast on what would have been a spectacular cake, and to bring her wedding bouquet to lay on Arthur's grave. She stares at his name on the marker and hears again his voice, sees his face. And suddenly she knows what she was waiting for.

She waves once more to the men in the truck, then goes to the car.

"I won six times," Nola tells her, and climbs over the front seat to get into her booster seat.

Matthew looks over at Maddy. "Ready?" he asks quietly.

"Yes. All buckled in, Nola?"

The little girl nods, and stares out the window. "Those men are putting dirt on Grandma Lucille."

"Yes," Maddy says. She's not quite sure what to say. She tries, "Now Grandma will be all cozy and tucked away."

Nola seems to buy it, for she says, "And we can visit her whenever we want."

"That's right." Maddy tightens her coat collar around her neck. To Matthew, she says, "Let's go and see if anyone came back to the house. And then I want to talk to you about something."

When they turn the corner onto Lucille's street,

they are surprised to find that parked cars line both sides of the street. Once they get into the house, Maddy has to push through a crowd to find Iris.

"Who are all these people?" she asks.

"Students," Iris says. "I think anyone who ever took a class has come. Did you see the dining room table?"

Maddy shakes her head no.

"Go and look," Iris says. "I've got to start another pot of coffee."

Maddy goes into the dining room, where Matthew and Nola have already gone. There is no room for anything else on the expanded table: the entire surface is covered with beautiful baked goods. Maddy recognizes Lucille's orange cake, her cinnamon rolls, her mile-high apple pie. Cookies, bars, tea breads, coffee cakes, cobblers. A thirtysomething woman Maddy doesn't recognize calls her name, and Maddy walks over. The woman is wearing a black dress, over which is an apron. And now that Maddy looks again, she sees aprons everywhere. They are Lucille's aprons: Maddy sees the lace apron, the ruffled apron, gingham aprons, organza "company" aprons, the apron with embroidered bluebirds, the one with floating rolling pins, several in pastel colors with wide rickrack. This woman is wearing the Paris apron with the French poodles.

She introduces herself to Maddy. "I'm Gwen Johnson. I took three of Lucille's classes, and it changed my life. Really! My whole approach to cooking and eating changed because of her. She practically saved my family life—we were all drifting apart and didn't really know it. I got into cooking because of Lucille, and my husband and our kids and I began eating together far more often, and what a difference! When I read in the paper that Lucille had died, I thought it would be a nice tribute if a bunch of us who took her classes got together to bring over something that she taught us to make."

"She would have been so honored," Maddy says.

"And she would have called out every mistake!" Gwen says, laughing. "But you know, you learned pretty fast not to be offended by Lucille. Because at heart . . ."

Maddy smiles. "Yes." And then, to Nola, who is doing an admirable job of stacking treats high on her plate, "Nola! That's enough!"

Nola stands still, regarding her mother from the corner of her eyes, which means she's debating whether or not to obey her. "Only two more?" she asks.

Oh, why not. Nothing like a funeral to loosen the rules. "All right," Maddy says. "Go ahead."

And then, meeting Matthew's eyes, she gestures for him to come with her out of the room. She'll tell him her idea in private, and see what he thinks.

# Onward

———

"WHAT'S GOING ON NEXT DOOR?" ABBY ASKS, as she comes into the kitchen. She's looking out the window into Lucille's kitchen, where many people are moving about.

"It's a lunch for Lucille," Jason says.

Abby comes to sit at the table. She's still weak, and she certainly seems to need a lot of sleep, but she's got her appetite back. On the table is a platter of cinnamon rolls with thick white icing. Abby smiles. "Really?"

Jason nods. "Once a month, okay?"

"Once a week," she says, after taking a bite. She looks out the window again. "I'm surprised they didn't invite us."

"They did."

Abby stops chewing.

"I thought it might be too much for you," Jason says. "And I was afraid of upsetting Link."

"Did you ask him?"

"No."

"Link!" Abby calls.

A faint "Yeah?"

"Can you come downstairs?"

Link comes downstairs and over to the table. "What's up?"

"Would you like to go next door to the lunch they're having for Lucille?"

He nods. "I made a card for her. I mean, you know, in her honor."

"May I see it?"

"Yeah. I'll get it."

He goes back upstairs and Abby looks at Jason.

"You were right," he says. "He wants to go."

"And I do, too." She takes Jason's hand. "We've been talking a lot, Link and I. You know?"

He overheard them once. Abby was saying that all her illness had done was to make her love Link and Daddy more. And appreciate everything more. And to understand, in a way she never had before, that death was a natural part of life, just like the seasons in nature. And everybody's job was to love life while you had it and never to take anything for granted. It was hard to remember to do that, but it was worth it to try. It was quiet, and then Link said, "Mom. Look. There's a cardinal right outside the window."

"I see him, sweetheart," Abby said. "Shall we watch him for a while?"

When Link comes back to the table, he shows them the card. On the front, he has drawn a cuckoo clock, the little door open, the bird's announcement being made and made. Inside, he has written, **Thanks for everything. With love from your friend, Link.**

"This is very nice," Abby says. "Let me get dressed and we'll all go over together."

She looks over at Jason, who smiles. Okay, then. Onward.

# An Odd Request

⸻

ON MONDAY MORNING, TERESA MCDOUGAL, Mason's town clerk, receives a call that gives her pause. It's enough of a pause that the caller finally says, "Hello? Are you there?"

"Yes, I'm here," she says. "I just . . . Well, I've never had a request like that. I'm going to have to ask the cemetery committee. Give me your number, and I'll call you back."

She writes down the number, hangs up the phone, and then stares into space for a moment. Here's tonight's topic of conversation at the dinner table, that's for sure!

She pushes back from her desk, leaving a newly poured cup of coffee in favor of a more interesting proposition. Bud Nelson, who is an alderman on the cemetery committee, is in his office.

"Hey, Bud," Teresa says, knocking on his door-frame, "have you got a minute?"

"Just about a minute. I forgot something I need for our meeting tonight and then I've got to get to work." He tightens his skinny tie: Bud hasn't changed his style of ties in more than fifty years. Or his style of glasses. He always says what's out will come back in again, and why should he waste the money. And he's right. Everything once dorky can become coolly ironic. To Teresa, Bud looks like that musician Elvis Costello.

"I just got a call," Teresa says. "Do we allow people to get married in cemeteries?"

Bud stares at her. "Come again?"

"I just got a call from a young lady who wants to get married in the cemetery."

"Whatever for?"

"She says it's an important place for her. She wants to get married on that little hill by the pond, where the willow tree is, you know the spot?"

"Sure I do. It's a nice spot. For reflection. For contemplation. But not for a wedding, for Pete's sake!"

"She says it will be very small, just her, the groom, her father, her daughter, and two witnesses. They'll be in and out. No muss, no fuss. She just wants to stand on that hill and get married. I mean, it's odd, but do you think it will hurt anything?"

"Well, I don't know. That's the question, isn't it? Let me ask the committee. I would think someone would need to be there, to supervise."

Teresa raised her hand. "I will. I'm curious!"

Bud nods. "Tell you what, if the committee agrees, I'll go with you. I'm curious myself."

THE NEXT MORNING, TERESA gets a call from Bud, who says, "All right, we made a decision. We'll meet with the couple, and if they're not . . . well, if they're not wisenheimers or some such thing, we'll let them do it. But that's it. One time. We can't be opening the floodgates for people to do what-all in what is, after all, a sacred space."

"Oh, I'm so glad," Teresa says. She is. And she is hard-pressed to say why. Something in that young woman's voice.

My goodness. Maybe she'll bring her Albert along. When she told him about the request last night, he was full of questions she couldn't answer. All she knew was that the caller, whose name was Maddy Harris, was someone who'd known Arthur Moses, the former groundskeeper for the parks. He was just the kindest man, and he used to carry butterscotch candies in his pocket to give to little kids. Although Teresa was known to have one of those candies every now and then herself.

# The Night Before

═══

"MORE WINE, ANYONE?" MONICA ASKS, and Nola says, "Me."

Maddy gives her daughter a look.

"Everybody gets some but me?"

"Right. Everybody gets some but you. Because you're a child."

The women are sitting in a circle on the floor of the living room of Lucille's house, passing around a good bottle of red. Lucille had told Nola that a bride must under no circumstances see her groom the night before the wedding, and Nola insisted that the dictum be honored, so here they are, Iris, Monica, Maddy, and Nola. Tiny and Matthew are out at the Alarm Bell before they journey on to who knows where. Nola is in her pajamas, the women are still in the clothes they wore out to dinner, but all of them are sleeping here tonight. Tomorrow, they will help Maddy get ready for the ceremony.

"Little French kids drink wine," Nola says.

"Who told you that?" her mother asks.

"I don't remember," Nola says diplomatically, but her eyes slide over to Monica.

"Well," Monica says quickly, "they do, but they're French, right? Different cultures do different things. For example, did you know that in Germany, it is a tradition for the just-marrieds to saw a log in half together in front of all their guests?"

"What for?" asks Maddy.

"It's to show that they're ready to work together to face the difficulties that may come in their marriage."

"**May** come?" Iris says. "Ha!"

"Now, now," Maddy says. "Don't jinx me."

"What does 'jinx' mean?" Nola asks.

"To bring bad luck to something," Maddy says. "For weddings, there are traditions to keep away bad luck. But they're really just for fun. You know how we talked about how, on your wedding day, you should wear something old, something new, something borrowed, and something blue?"

"**Why,** though?"

Maddy fills her glass again. "Actually, I don't know, either."

"I do!" Monica says. "I'm the encyclopedia of weddings. Something old is to represent the bride's past, and the new is for the couple's future. Something borrowed is supposed to come from someone who has a happy marriage, so their good fortune will rub off. Something blue—"

"Is for the sad times," says Maddy.

"Nope. It's to represent fidelity and love. Chinese brides wear red for fertility."

"What's fertility?" asks Nola.

"Having children," Maddy tells her.

Nola's eyes widen. "Are you going to have more children?"

"I hadn't thought of it," Maddy says. "Would you like a brother or a sister?"

"No!"

The women laugh.

Iris says, "I had a college roommate from Kenya, and she told me that there, when the newlyweds leave the village, the father of the bride spits on his daughter's head and chest so as not to jinx their good fortune."

"That doesn't even make any sense," Monica says. She is slouching low against the sofa, and one shoe is off. She had two martinis at the restaurant, generously poured.

"Okay, here's a really nice one," Monica says. "In Australia, they have what's called a Unity Bowl. And all the guests are given stones and told to hold them during the ceremony. Afterward, they put them all in a bowl that the couple keep and display to remember the support and blessings of their friends."

Maddy looks at her watch, then at Nola. "Bedtime. Go on up and I'll check in on you in a little bit, okay?"

"I'm not tired," Nola says. But she gives all the women a kiss and then heads for the stairs. "Good night," she calls, and the women all call back, "Good niiiight!" Maddy loves hearing the singsong quality of the women's voices. They are mothers' voices, irrespective of the fact that Maddy is the only one with a child.

"A good-night kiss" sounds like a little poem to Maddy. As a child, she never got good-night kisses. She tried once, she kissed her father good night when she was around three, and he endured it—sat unsmiling and stiff as a stone, his arms at his side—and then said, "Okay, that's enough, go to bed." She never tried again. But now! Let it never be said that Nola was not given good-night kisses. Let it never be said that she didn't practically drown in them.

Monica belches and quietly excuses herself; there is the sound of Nola's feet racing down the hall to her bedroom. And then: nothing. Peace.

Then Monica says, "Oh, Lord. I can't believe it. I think I'm going to be sick. Oh, gosh, I'm so embarr—"

She races off to the downstairs bathroom, there is the sound of muffled retching, and then Maddy and Iris decide maybe they'll go to bed, too.

After Maddy turns out the light, she lies with her eyes open, worrying. Is it normal for brides to second-guess themselves the night before their wedding? She can't help but wonder if this was a good idea, after all. Oh, she loves Matthew, but . . . what is marriage, anyway? What will it confer upon her that she doesn't have now? She doesn't plan on having more children. She wants a great deal of freedom. What if she marries Matthew and things turn sour? What if she ends up divorced and has to put Nola through that? What if she said she wanted a divorce and Nola said she wanted to live with Matthew?

Maddy goes over to the window, a pink-and-white quilt that Lucille made wrapped around her. Outside, the stars are clear behind the thin cloud cover and the moon is full, making it look like daynight outside. Nola's term, **daynight**. Nola's perception that at sunset, **the sky comes down.**

Maddy leans her forehead against the glass. This was Lucille's bedroom window. She wonders now if Lucille ever even looked out of it. Lucille was so purpose-driven. It seemed like she woke up every morning with a list in her head that she started working on the moment her feet hit the floor. It's hard for Maddy to imagine that Lucille ever engaged in much self-reflection, much less self-doubt, which is Maddy's specialty, even now, even after all the changes she's made in her life. What Maddy has come to believe is that certain life circumstances make for people who walk with a psychic limp for all of their days. Never mind the progress they seem to make, peel back a few delicate layers and there it is: a stubborn doubting of worth; an inability to stand with conviction behind anything without wondering if they should be standing there at all; a sense that if they move in this direction, it's wrong; and if they move in that direction, that's wrong, too. As for

Maddy, there are only two places where she feels rooted in surety: in her work, and in the caretaking of her daughter.

Maddy has told Matthew all of this; she has told him she's not sure she can be counted on to be reliable in a relationship. She's told him she's not sure she really believes in marriage. Furthermore, she's said that she's not sure that when you say you love someone, you're not just saying that you love yourself in his image.

But Matthew wants to marry her anyway. "I know you may not stay with me forever," he said just last night, "but I'm so grateful to have you now, and for as long as you can stay." Which naturally made her wish she could stay with him forever.

Of course, he could change his mind—wouldn't that be ironic? He could come to her someday and say, "Maddy, I'm sorry, but we need to talk."

She walks over to the other window, looks out at the street below, at the bare branches of the rosebushes that Arthur planted. She supposes he planted them for his own pleasure but also for his wife's. Now, there was a love story, Arthur and his wife, Nola. It seemed like they were so happy, so content. But then Arthur could never fight with anyone, and he forgave everything. Even so, Maddy supposes that even in what appeared to be their near-perfect relationship there were cracks and fissures.

She goes back to the bed and sits on the edge, pulling the quilt tighter around her shoulders and rocking, slowly at first, then faster and faster. **"Stop,"** she whispers.

Just then a warmth comes into her and she very nearly feels his presence, sees his brown eyes, his wire-hanger shoulders, his stick-out ears and long, skinny legs. "Arthur?" she says out loud, feeling only a little foolish. And then she gives herself over to the conversation that comes to her.

"Nervous, huh?" he asks.

"Yes."

"Everybody will tell you that's natural. But on my wedding day, it didn't feel natural to me. No, sir. I kept thinking, **What is the matter with you? You're the man, the strong one, the one who knew right away she was the one, why, your first words to her were that you were going to marry her. And now you're shaking like a leaf.** Which I was, Maddy, my hands were shaking so bad I couldn't pour myself a cup of coffee.

"All during the ceremony I tried not to give anything away, but do you know when it came time to kiss the bride, I missed the mark and kissed her nose! And that night, when she went into the bathroom to change and I lay under the bedcovers, I thought I might plumb pass out. But then she came out and she was a vision in blue. A real vision, her hair loosened from her fancy 'do, no makeup, just her beautiful plain face there, her skin as soft as flower petals, her eyes like a calm pool. She sat at the edge of the bed and she took my hand and she said, 'Do you think I don't know you're scared about every-thing?' Oh, I felt so found out. I said, 'Are you?' 'Not one bit,' she said. She was always the strong one, Nola. And that night she asked me to tell her what I was afraid of, and I did. Not just the manly task before me, but marriage itself. I confessed everything to her. I saw that there was going to be no pretend-ing in our marriage. And that in accepting my weakness, she made us both strong. And then she lay beside me and said, 'We have all the time in the world, Arthur.' Well, I knew we didn't have all he time in the world. I knew we were mortals slated to a short life at its longest. But I loved her to the tip-top every day of our lives together. And every day after she died, I loved her that way still, no difference."

"I know," Maddy says. "That's why I named you Truluv."

"I'll tell you something, Maddy. Half of a good marriage is having someone love you for who you really are. You've got that already. The other half is both of you making a commitment to stay together not only at the altar but smack dab in the middle of every ugly fight. One time when Nola and I were really going at it, I walked over and kissed her hard. And she kissed me back. And then, why, we went right back at it and finished the argument. And I'd guess she won it, she won most of them, fair and square.

"Marriage is like weather, Maddy. You take it day by day. You rejoice in the good days and get through the bad ones, though I don't think you'll have many bad ones because you found an ace of a fellow. But you go ahead and be as nervous as you need to be. A little nervousness never hurt anyone."

Maddy takes in a deep breath. She throws the pillow back onto the bed and tiptoes down the hall to Nola's room. The child is a messy sleeper; covers and body parts go every which way. Her face twitches, and Maddy wonders if she is dreaming, and, if so, what she is dreaming about. Life is an ongoing adventure for Nola. She is strong and she is happy and she seems to like herself just fine. So . . . so there.

When Maddy heads back down the hall to go to bed, she hears the voices of Monica and Iris, who are downstairs, Monica on the sofa, Iris on the sofa cushions that have been put on the floor.

"But would you ever do it again?" Monica asks.

"No," Iris says. "I don't think so."

"But maybe?"

Iris laughs. "Okay. Yes. Maybe."

**They're talking about marriage,** Maddy thinks. But then she hears Monica say, "What about in a swimming pool? Did you ever do it there?"

"No," Iris says.

"In a shower?" Monica says.

"Nope."

"Well, hell," Monica says. "No wonder you got divorced."

Maddy laughs, and they hear her and call for her to come down to be with them, and she does.

# Here Comes the Bride

J UST BEFORE IT'S TIME TO LEAVE FOR THE CERE-
mony, Maddy is sitting in Arthur's old bedroom.
She hasn't slept much, but she doesn't feel tired. She's
thinking about Arthur and Lucille. She misses them
all the time, really, but today their absence is keenly
felt.

The door pushes in and Nola appears, wearing a
colander on her head. "This is my crown," she says.

"Very nice," Maddy tells her.

"If you **really** think it is nice, you may wear it to
your **wedding**!" Then, stepping closer to her mother,
"What's wrong?"

Before Nola was born, Maddy promised herself to
speak the truth to her child. And so she says, "I'm
kind of missing Lucille and Arthur."

"Well," Nola says, "I know of a thing that is very
good in life."

"What?"

"Fish."

"To eat?"

"No, silly! To swim!"

"Oh. Well, they are beautiful, aren't they?"

"No, but it's that they swim and swim and they don't even have to come up for air."

"True."

Nola spins around and around, her arms out at her side. "I will say that at your wedding!"

Half an hour later, Maddy arrives at the cemetery and asks for a few moments alone. She goes to stand before Lucille's grave, coatless. The December day is mild, but not enough to be without a coat. Still, for just a few minutes, Maddy wants to be revealed as the resplendent bride that she is. She is wearing an Art Deco gown that Iris helped her find on Etsy, something from the thirties. It's very simple, close-fitting, many buttons on the sleeves. There's a bias-cut godet in the front skirt, and two long sashes that tie on the left side. The color is a deep ivory that leans toward yellow; it makes it look as though the gown is infused with sun. The silk fabric feels like heavy water in the hands.

Maddy closes her eyes and offers a kind of thanks to Lucille, then goes to Arthur's grave and does the same thing.

Now she looks over at the little hill where Matthew waits for her, Matthew and Nola and Maddy's father, and Monica and Tiny, who are serving as witnesses. Off to the side are three other figures, two men and a woman, whom she suspects are from the cemetery committee: she was told someone would be there. They're huddled together, and even from here, Maddy can see that they seem even more excited than she is: arms pressed into their sides, necks craned, big smiles plastered on their faces. The woman has on a fancy hat, and a big corsage pinned to her coat. One of the men is wearing an old fedora that under other circumstances Maddy would ask to photograph.

She takes her place beside Matthew and nods at Jon Brand, a friend who has recently become ordained as a minister. He's an English professor at the college where Maddy went to school and where Matthew taught, and he shares with Maddy a great love of poetry. Today, he reads two poems that Maddy requested, Jane Hirshfield's "A Blessing for Wedding," and Robert Frost's "Birches." She selected them because she believes now—finally—that earth **is** "the right place for love." And she does indeed wish for the vastness of the vows exchanged today to be ever "undisguised."

Maddy turns to her daughter. "Nola, did you want to say anything?"

Nola, holding Monica's hand, stares wide-eyed at her mother, then up at Monica.

"No?" Maddy asks.

Nola shakes her head.

"All right, then." Maddy turns back to face the minister.

"Fish!" Nola says. "Are good in life!"

Maddy tells her daughter thank you, and on the little hill near the pond and the willow tree, where a younger Maddy once lay, aching and unmoored and isolated in a way that she thought would last forever, she is proven happily wrong.

When Maddy closes her eyes to receive a kiss from her husband, she feels hand-size points of warmth on each of her shoulders. Maybe they are from her husband's hands. Maybe not.

# Fun as a Jigsaw!

═══

IRIS SITS IN LUCILLE'S KITCHEN SCOWLING AT the computer screen. She skipped the ceremony to stay behind and finish the cake. Maddy wanted chocolate and vanilla, so Iris is watching a YouTube video on how to assemble a checkerboard cake. She'd found a recipe for one on a three-by-five index card stuck into one of Lucille's many cake cookbooks. The instructions for baking the four cakes were clear enough, two chocolate, two vanilla, and that's all done—she finished that early this morning. But for the assembly, here was what Lucille had written: **Construct in usual way.**

Iris watches as the cheerful woman on the screen says, "It's so much fun doing this, it's like putting together a jigsaw puzzle!" Iris doesn't like jigsaw puzzles. Not now, not ever. She finds even easy puzzles difficult, and for the life of her, just doesn't see the point in laboring over them. For one thing, when you have finished, what do you have? What are you going to do with it? Take it apart again, that's what. Puzzle aficionados have tried to explain their appeal, but it is ever lost on Iris.

Never mind. She leans forward, grits her teeth, squints her eyes, and watches the video one more time. She thinks she understands, but maybe she'll have a trial run with Styrofoam. When she looks at her watch, though, she sees she's out of time. She'll have to dive right in in order to have the cake ready for the reception.

She puts on one of Lucille's aprons, and closes her eyes; she can smell Lucille's old-timey lilac perfume on it. In her head, Lucille is bustling about with her, talking fast, like she always did when she got excited. **Now, remember: if you're afraid, the cake will take advantage. Act like you know what you're doing, see? All you're doing is making a cake. Making a cake! What could be easier? Now get going; it needs to be perfect.**

In only fifteen minutes, the cake is done, and Iris is enormously proud. She takes a picture of it. What she wants to do is text the image to Lucille, who never even had a cellphone and who is dead, besides. Never mind. She "texts" it to Lucille; it's an "alternative" text. Then she sends a real text with the photo to Tiny. **Just leaving the cemetery**, he texts back. **Cake is awedome!** She knows what he means. In more ways than one. The cake is spectacular. She can't wait to serve it, and she realizes that she has found her next calling. She will take Maddy up on her offer to rent Lucille's house. She will continue to teach baking here, not as the expert Lucille was, not at first, but maybe eventually. In any case, the beat will go on. So to speak. Iris smiles, thinking of Lucille's insistence on beating so many things by hand. So often when she seemed persnickety, she was only right.

# A Little Town

---

MASON LOOKS GOLDEN-RED IN THE LIGHT OF the sun coming up on a late January day. Not much is stirring; the quiet is like a blanket. The snow is melting, and birds hopping about in it have made hieroglyphical indentations. Here and there, on people's front lawns, are various-size snowmen, listing in one direction or another, like carrot-nosed drunks welcoming visitors. This day will be even warmer than yesterday, never mind the deeper march into winter; mittens and scarves will be left behind on playgrounds.

Outside Sugarbutter bakery, a man loads bread onto a truck. Newspapers are thrown onto porches with a satisfying **thwack.** Nurses change shifts, cops, too. Roberto starts the coffeemakers at the Henhouse, the grill gets heated up.

Abby and Jason lie awake in their bed, but feign

sleep so as not to disturb each other so early in the morning. They will have a busy day today; it's the grand opening of Menagerie Bookshop, the store they're opening, complete with dog, cat, parakeet, and goldfish. Lincoln brought Hope into bed with him in the night, as he does every night, and the dog snores her funny snore. Monica and Tiny sleep curled around each other, wedding rings bright on their hands. Iris is up early in her kitchen, preparing for the "Lemon-ganza" class she is teaching this afternoon: four women and one man will be making lemon bars, lemon meringue pie, and gingerbread with an exquisite warm lemon-butter sauce.

Lucille's alarm clock, stationed now at Iris's bedside, glows in the relative darkness, but soon the moving hands will be clearly seen and there will be no need for artificial light.

YOU ARE SEATED BY CHOICE OR MISFORTUNE in a window seat on an airplane. You look out as the plane takes off, rises up higher and higher, levels off. If you chance to glance down, you see a particular kind of order not realized on earth. You might feel a kind of hopefulness at the sight of houses clustered together in their various neighborhoods, at roads running straight or artfully curved, at what look like toy cars. You see the lakes and rivers, occasionally the wide stretch of ocean meeting horizon. You see natural quilts formed by the lay of fields and farmlands, you see the grouping of trees into parks and forests. Sometimes you see the splendor of autumn leaves or Fourth of July fireworks. Or sunsets. Or sunrises.

All of this can inspire something unnameable but nearly graspable, a kind of yearning toward a grand possibility.

Then you land.

And you know something. You can feel it. It's right there.

# ACKNOWLEDGMENTS

I once wrote a children's book called **Ralph Anderson's Pretty Good Birthday,** about a dog who was having a swell birthday until a cat came along. I wrote it on ivory-colored, pulpy paper, illustrated it with crayons, took full advantage of my stapler and Scotch tape dispenser for the "binding," and presented it to my young daughters. This meant that the reading audience for my book was three, and my payment nothing.

Were it not for the people I want to acknowledge here, I suspect my process would still be much the same.

Kate Medina is the editor who believed in me from day one. Let me tell you a story about her. When we first met, she had read the partial manuscript for my first novel and thought she wanted to buy it. She did have one question: What was going to happen at the end of the book? I didn't know. I tried to answer, but I didn't know. And so I said, "I don't think I can talk about that." Before the words were fully out of my mouth, she waved her hand and said, "Fine." And that's when I knew she was the editor for me. Not only does Kate know and understand writers, she respects their weird ways. She makes me feel like I'm her only author, too. It's a miracle. When I think about what I am most grateful for in my writing life, Kate Medina is at the top of the list.

Kate has an assistant named Erica Gonzalez, who is the soul of patience and kindness and accommodation. I am grateful to her for favors both large and small, and though I wish her great success in the industry, I hope she stays where she is for a long time.

One of the things I enjoy most in the final stages of having a novel published is working with production editor extraordinaire Beth Pearson. She makes finding the best word or phrase so much fun. Exciting, even. And I trust her judgement implicitly. Thanks, Beth, for your many years of working with me, and for all the help you've given me.

I am an author who is perhaps overly invested in her cover art, and I am also an author who is blessed to work with Paolo Pepe on my jacket designs. He doesn't just say he is open to my opinion, he really is open to my opinion. Also, the man knows what he is doing. I am so lucky that he is on my team, and I always look forward to seeing what he comes up with. Thanks, too, to Barbara Bachman, for the book's interior design.

Christine Mykityshyn, in publicity, is the consummate professional, and just a really nice person to boot. Her assistant, Stephanie Reddaway, is indispensable in helping to craft a book tour, and she responds to emails lickety-split, no small feat.

When the writing's done and the book is ready to meet the world, I am so happy to have Avideh Bashirrad, Leigh Marchant, and Andrea DeWerd in charge of the voodoo that they do. I owe you each a dozen of Lucille's best cookies. Please put in your requests soon so I know how much high-fat butter to buy.

Benjamin Dreyer, you are a continual source of comfort, and a class act. Thank you.

Many sparkly thanks to Suzanne Gluck, my agent, for her expertise and honesty and good ideas, and for being a partner in crime for the Lucy-and-Ethel escapades.

Bill Young: Love and thanks for a gazillion things, including walking the dog in winter.

Speaking of dogs, to Gabby: You really **are** a good girl. The best girl.

To my writing group, Veronica Chapa, Arlene Malinowsky, Marja Mills, Pam Todd, Michele Weldon (and Phyllis Florin, in absentia): Whew, you save me from myself.

Last, but certainly not least, thank you to every single reader who lets me know that my message is being heard and appreciated. You make my days.

# ABOUT THE AUTHOR

ELIZABETH BERG is the author of many bestselling novels, including **The Story of Arthur Truluv, Open House** (an Oprah's Book Club selection), **Talk Before Sleep,** and **The Year of Pleasures,** as well as the short story collection **The Day I Ate Whatever I Wanted. Durable Goods** and **Joy School** were selected as ALA Best Books of the Year. She adapted **The Pull of the Moon** into a play that enjoyed sold-out performances in Chicago and Indianapolis. Berg's work has been published in thirty countries, and three of her novels have been turned into television movies. She is the founder of Writing Matters, a quality reading series dedicated to serving author, audience, and community. She teaches one-day writing workshops and is a popular speaker at venues around the country. Some of her favorite Facebook postings have been collected in **Make Someone Happy** and **Still Happy.** She lives outside Chicago.

elizabeth-berg.net
Facebook.com/bergbooks

# LIKE WHAT YOU'VE READ?

If you enjoyed this large print edition of
**NIGHT OF MIRACLES**,
here are two of Elizabeth Berg's latest
bestsellers also available in large print.

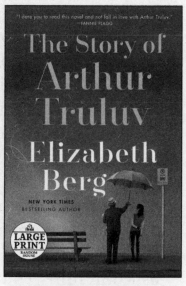

**Once Upon a Time,
There Was You**
(paperback)
978-0-7393-7813-7
($26.00/$30.00 CAN)

**The Story of Arthur Truluv**
(paperback)
978-1-5247-8303-7
($28.00/$37.00 CAN)

Large print books are available wherever books
are sold and at many local libraries.

All prices are subject to change. Check with your
local retailer for current pricing and availability.
For more information on these and other large print titles, visit:
**www.penguinrandomhouse.com/large-print-format-books**